Son of Asmodeus

Heaven and Hell

Barb Jones

DEDICATION

Arianna and Kaiden: Always for you. Because of you.

Mom: For your continuing support and love for everything I do.

Frank Lang: For being the best friend I could ever hope for, cheering me on to go after my dreams.

To My Beta Read Team: Thank you for helping make this come to life with all your input.

"A person often meets his destiny on the road he took to avoid it."
Jean de la Fontaine

OTHER WORKS BY BARB JONES

BLOOD PROPHECY SERIES
QUEEN'S DESTINY
QUEEN'S ENEMY
QUEEN'S ASCENSION

BLOOD PROPHECY NOVELLAS
AMBER: BIRTH OF A QUEEN
CHLOE: VISIONS OF THE FUTURE
MARCUS: ORIGINS
MACHIEL: STONE OF THE DAMNED
ZARAQUEL: MORAL COMPASS

HENRY AND ANNE: A TUDOR LOVE STORY

COMING SOON

BLOOD PROPHECY II
RISE OF THE HUNTER

THE DEVIL INSIDE ME

HEAVEN AND HELL SERIES
HELL HOUNDS

PROLOGUE

The Pact

Outside the throne room doors, a war raged between angels and demons. As the archangel Michael killed several demons, his eyes were locked on a demon prince named Balam. Balam hurled an angel against the rock and was prepared to strike again. He noticed Balam was watching him as if he was the next target. Michael was too occupied with a different demon, Beelzebub, to help the fallen angel or deal with the demon prince.

Michael prepared to kill Beelzebub with his heavenly sword but was soon overpowered when a smaller demon snuck up behind him, jumping on his back. He dropped his sword and fought with his hands. Michael's blonde hair was streaked with demon blood from the previous kills while smudges of blood stained his beautiful, high cheekbones. His golden wings were stained with blood as well. The demon made a slight tear in one of his wings in the surprise attack. The walls shook as a loud voice was heard, causing everyone to stop fighting.

"There will be no fighting inside the gates of Heaven. I command you, Lucifer, to leave at once or I will take your life. I made all that is before me, including you. I have the power to destroy what I have created. The two kingdoms will not fight in my kingdom."

Michael looked at Balam, who hung his head in defeat and left. The demon who attacked him followed. He noticed that demon after demon was leaving, including their master, Lucifer. Angels lay motionless and Michael's heart broke. He ordered those who were still standing to take the angels' bodies away. Michael found the archangel Raphael and pulled him aside.

They sat alone in the empty throne room, contemplating the battle that had just happened as well as the Lord's command. Michael slammed both hands on the table in a rage at the damage done to his brothers and sisters, not to mention the disarray the throne room was in. They needed to find a way to spare each kingdom a significant defeat that would eradicate the world that the Lord, their Creator, had fashioned in his image.

Michael was frustrated and angry that the Lord and Lucifer didn't want to reconcile. His brother, Lucifer, refused to return home. He wanted peace, but at what cost to both the Lord and the angels? The Lord had made it clear to everyone in the room that he could eliminate Lucifer and possibly others if this rage for domination continued, and Michael was torn at the thought of losing another brother or sister. As a result, the kingdoms of Heaven and Hell were divided and the gates to each were closed to the other, causing continuous battles between the angels and the demons There was no other option since Lucifer refused reconciliation

"Michael, brother, we can't continue to watch our brothers and sisters die. My heart is breaking."

"I know. As I sit here, I wonder what our Lord would allow us to do to save the kingdoms, let alone his children of the world."

Michael noticed that he wasn't the only one in a foul mood. Raphael was hurt, broken, and upset because of the fighting and death that had been brought into Heaven. As they sat in silence, another angel came running into the room, sounding the alarm that a large demon faction, sent by Lucifer, had returned for another fight. Michael was in disarray considering the Lord had just issued the ultimatum to Lucifer but he trusted the news. This angel was one of the Lord's favorites. Jophiel. Beautiful, sweet, and kind. Her dark hair was long, and her choice of weapon was a flaming sword that Michael had given to her for justice. She held onto it while trying to shut the doors. A horde of demons broke through, breaking the wood into pieces and sending Jophiel backwards until she fluttered her wings to rise in the air. A great defeat for Heaven. The passage was vulnerable as the horde came through. One battle just ended only to begin again within moments of Lucifer's departure. Something was seriously wrong with that fallen angel.

Standing up, he called upon his trusted sword and sought revenge against the fallen angels who entered. The demons were no longer welcome into the kingdom of Heaven. Michael raised his sword into the air and called upon the flames of justice. He pointed the sword at the demon horde, making his intention known to all in the room. Michael lunged toward one, slashing him into two halves with one strike. On another demon, he used the flames from his sword to burn him. Michael found himself encircled by five demons while Jophiel was cornered by Lucifer. Raphael was in his own predicament as well with several of the enemy attacking his sword.

He raised his sword once more and said, "Flames of Heavenly Justice, I command you to strike."

As his sword lit up in flames, he pointed the tip of the blade toward the demons that encircled him and watched as their flesh was consumed. He pointed at the demons that kept Raphael occupied and, using his weapon, he freed Raphael while setting the demons on fire. As for Lucifer, he pointed the sword at him, and a circle of fire formed by his feet, allowing Jophiel to use her wings to find her way toward Raphael. Then he commanded the flames to disappear.

"Impressive, Michael. Can you defeat me, the King of Hell, and save your kingdom? I should think not, favorite son of our Father."

Michael smiled and pointed his sword at him. Lucifer was grinning. Something was amiss. Michael had killed his horde and yet he didn't react. Lucifer, with his sword in hand, moved closer but maintained his distance. Michael expected him to lunge toward him, but he didn't. He inched closer, savoring each step. As he made his way towards Lucifer, he commanded anyone else in the room to leave the two alone.

Standing face to face with his Lord's enemy, a power of grace came over him, granting him confidence in besting this fallen angel. Lucifer had changed little since he fell from grace. He still had the scar that Michael had given him on his cheek for turning his back on the Lord. He was still as beautiful as before, despite his scar. His short, dark hair was the same, except for the hair that now adorned his face. As Lucifer smiled, Michael leaped up into the air and moved with an air of confidence about him. His great wings fluttered, giving him the speed and agility he needed. Lucifer was always the stronger one when they'd practiced together a long time ago.

Lucifer made a great leap, using his black wings, and tried to pull Michael down. Michael moved away and with a flick of his wrist, cut into Lucifer's shoulder, leaving a deep gash. Once Lucifer fell to the ground, he dusted off and lunged again. Anticipating Lucifer's move, Michael moved to the left, avoiding his powerful blow.

He continued to frustrate Lucifer with several surprising moves, causing him to grow angrier each time.

"Brother, you have been practicing."

Michael kneeled with his head bowed in prayer but made sure he could see Lucifer in case he moved.

Lucifer moved behind Michael, but he felt the fallen angel near him, gripping his hand tighter on his magnificent sword. He pulled his arm back and let the blade cut Lucifer once more, this time injuring his side. He watched as Lucifer fled the throne room. Once he was gone, Michael sealed the doors and the passage to Heaven before calling Raphael to join him.

"Come, Raphael, I have a plan. I have need of you because you have the power to guard pilgrims on their journeys. I need a prophet to be the pilgrim and this plan is one that requires a sacrifice by Heaven and Hell. No one must know but you, me, our Lord, and Lucifer. And it will require a price to be paid by each kingdom. It might just work if you would let me use one of your prophets. However, we must deal with the current situation of our fallen brothers and sisters from this war. The passage must never fall again, especially to demons."

Michael didn't know if Raphael would take part or if he was just annoyed. There have been factions popping up in every corner and he was not yet convinced until Raphael extended his hand, offering it in agreement to send him Elias, the prophet. Michael left to speak to the Lord.

"Lord, I beseech you to end this battle with Lucifer. Your beautiful children, once angels but now demons, are dead because of this insanity. I have an idea if you'll listen to me."

The Lord was silent, nodding in agreement. Michael said he would take care of the details if they agreed on a pact. The Lord listened and agreed. Michael departed and called upon Lucifer.

Lucifer, reeling from the wounds inflicted upon him, listened to Michael. Lucifer agreed in kind, leaving Michael satisfied with his task. Both sides had lost significant numbers in angels and demons. Michael met with both the Lord and Lucifer present. In addition, he asked Lucifer to bring the demon prince Asmodeus, and he brought the archangel Jophiel as well. Raphael provided him with Elias.

Michael outlined his plan, calling upon Asmodeus and Jophiel to be willing partners. As everyone listened, a spark of interest ignited between the two that remained unseen by all except Michael. The pact was made.

Asmodeus and Jophiel were left alone to realize the depths of the pact that was intended by Michael all along.

Scottish Monastery—1329

The monk named Brother John sat writing in his journal, using a dimly lit candle so that his tired eyes could still see the parchment. It had been a long week for him, and he hoped for some rest.

Brother John remembered his childhood, filled with the stories that were told to him by his parents, even though they made little sense to him. He remembered those stories until he entered the monastery at age fourteen. His father would tell him how demons were once angels in heaven until they fell from grace. As he listened, his mother interjected with stories about archangels, especially Michael, and the heavenly gates. He loved hearing stories at night. After reflecting on his youth, Brother John continued to write, knowing this was his last entry. He heard the faint knock on the door. Grabbing his crucifix, he kissed it and placed it around his neck. He opened the door and nodded at the three monks and handed his journal to one of them for safekeeping.

They walked down the corridor in a somber silence. The monks were with him on his journey, but none could help him complete his task. They had trained him for only one purpose, though he learned other things from them that his own family would not share with him. He was like no other man. Brother John was a powerful exorcist. They never answered his simplest question about where he came from. It was always the same answer, year after year. *He was a special child with a unique purpose, adopted by parents that loved him.*

Now he was a man. Brother John always knew he was different and over time, no one appreciated him until he sought sanctuary here. As they walked, one monk handed him a rosary that he placed around his neck, while the other handed him a large wooden crucifix, his special bible, and holy water. Armed now with the tools that he needed, he reached the door at the end of the hallway. He looked out the window and took a deep breath. John knew the trees were there. He imagined the trees swaying in the breeze and the peacefulness of the forest that surrounded the monastery. This was his ultimate duty in the monastery and his service to the Lord.

The monks opened the large door. He ventured into

the room lit by candles. They drew a pentagram on the floor. The church forbade them from practicing demon craft, but there was no other choice. His aim was to protect humans. It was always up to him.

Inside the pentagram sat the child. He didn't look frightened or upset. His dark hair was tousled, in his nightclothes, ripped from his bed and brought to this room. The child had a crooked nose and bore the mark of Hell on his cheek. A symbol Brother John knew too well. He walked toward to child and noticed how the flames had cast their light on his face in the most haunted way. Brother John looked around and, searched for more light from the candles. He took a deep breath and prayed for forgiveness for once again breaking his vow of silence. They barricaded the door. They remained silent but acknowledged his sign of prayer for forgiveness.

Brother John had been doing this task of exorcism for many years. There was a child in the center. He couldn't cast out the demon despite his efforts. This child demon had taken what physical strength he had left. His spirit was the only weapon that wasn't broken. He looked at the others and noticed their facial expressions. Brother John could sense what people were feeling—there was fear in them. It was one thing that made him different.

The demon defeated him despite all his attempts from the past and now. He just couldn't exorcise this demon and it frustrated him to no end.

The child spoke. "Do you fear me, brother? Come closer, brother."

The facetiousness from the child annoyed Brother John. "Don't call me that. I serve the Lord and not your brother, spawn of evil. You are the vessel of the devil himself."

The child laughed and tried to move, which infuriated Brother John. The child loved his games. What came next blew Brother John away, and it was least unexpected.

"Have you ever wondered where you came from, brother? I know you feel different because I can sense what you feel. I know you can sense what I feel. Did you ever wonder why you can do these things? The training by your fellow monks was so specific. Why is that? They knew all along where you came from. Isn't that right, brother monks? Don't you think it is time my brother knew the truth of his origins, or do you want to continue to use him against his true nature?"

Brother John was confused, but he looked at the other monks. He knew they would never break their vow of silence for this. He noticed how they shifted in their stances as the child demon continued to stare at them. He asked God to forgive him as he poured the entire bottle of holy water on the child. Though the child screamed louder, it turned to taunting laughter.

The child twisted and contorted his little body in ways that made Brother John shudder. As he watched, he remained vigilant in his oath and purpose. The child was no better than the last time he tried to exorcise him. No matter the amount of prayer, he still resisted. Brother John approached the child and made the sign of the cross on him, but the child spat in his face. The child reached the boundary of the circle that kept him trapped and taunted him again.

"Brother John, solve this little riddle. Your blood is my blood. My story is your story. We both come from the same father. We are the products of the seed from one so foul, so wicked, that neither Heaven nor Hell knows what to do with us. Follow me and I will show you what it is you seek. Which demon is our father? How special are you, brother?"

Brother John placed the crucifix on the child's forehead, and he screamed again. There was no laughter, only the smell of burned flesh instead. The child turned towards the other monks and spoke in a very ancient language. The monks' flesh melted off their bodies, leaving a puddle on the floor. Brother John was terrified at that moment. The child demon had never retaliated like this. He wasn't certain where he came from. He felt a pull as if it was telling him to go. His will was strong, though he felt defeated. In the end, the pull won him over. He submitted.

He looked at the child and said, "I will follow you for the truth."

The child shared the secret with him. When he was done, Brother John's world was never the same.

CHAPTER 1

Los Angeles, Present Day (almost seven hundred years later)

John walked the streets of Sunset Boulevard every night, trying to forget his past, but a piece of it always found him. He never could shake the guilty feeling he'd felt since learning the truth from the child. He never believed a demon. This was a first. The church would call him to exorcise a demon. Or he would just find demons to kill. John was the demon hunter. Alone and always on guard.

John didn't want to be like his father if Edward's story was true. The child demon would always call him "brother." Despite being "brothers," Edward never opened up to him, which infuriated him, but the more he thought about it, perhaps it was because he was a demon hunter and Edward was a demon. After all, there were boundaries to the roles they played. The relationship was clear to him. He hunts. They die.

John was determined to be stronger in his faith since leaving the monastery. He served God by hunting demons. He never gave up on his oath. He was supported by the demon child until, one day, the child was gone without a word. Where he slept, John found a blade like no other. This became his hunting blade. He used it to kill demons, but he noticed a sense of fear in their eyes when they saw his blade. It was just one of many blades he used in his arsenal. He never paid much attention to the reason they feared it. He just wanted them dead.

In fact, he sensed a demon coming. Based on the foul and musty stench, he served Astaroth, one of the evil trinity next to Lucifer. John recognized that smell anywhere. He kept walking, waiting for the demon to get closer. John slowed his pace and felt in his pocket for his blade. Since he always wore his leather jacket, he could keep extra weapons hidden in the lining and pockets. Using his right hand, he made the sign of the cross and kissed the crucifix that always hung around his neck, a special gift all those years ago from his adopted mother. He found an alley and turned right, still waiting and listening for the demon to follow him.

There he was.

Glancing left to right, he surveyed the scene and made sure he was alone, or at least alone with the demon. Turning around, he stared into the demon's black eyes.

"Demon hunter."

"Prick," was all John had to say before the demon made the first strike.

As the demon punched John in the side of his face, he shook off the initial shock. Tasting a drop of blood from the corner of his mouth, John cocked his head to the left and then to the right while flexing his neck muscles. Before the demon could land a second blow, John pulled out his blade. The blade was black, cut uniquely, and the hilt bore symbols that were not known to many outside the inner circle of Hell. As he angled the blade to hit the light a bit more, the demon's eyes grew narrow.

John realized the demon was more afraid of the blade than him. He used that fear against the demon. He waved the blade, taunting his enemy. Tossing the blade from hand-to-hand excited John before the kill while he watched the demon's fear grow.

"You smell of Asteroth. What does he want with me? Do you like my toy? Want to play with it, prick?"

"Too many questions, hunter. Asteroth wants your head; then again, don't we all?" The demon snickered while shifting in his stance. "This body, do you like it, hunter? I thought it would be capable in killing you. This body is strong, hunter. Strong enough to kill you." The demon shifted in the body he possessed and then went to move closer to John.

John waved the blade around, either tempting the demon to play or making him angry. Either way, he made his point. He was the demon hunter. In the end, the demon would be dead. Life was beautiful when it went according to his plan, but this time it didn't.

The demon played and moved to get closer to John. John shifted in place, braced the weight of his legs against the pavement, and stood firm. The demon shoved him, though John did not move or lose his balance, but dropped the blade. The demon shoved him again, to no avail. John grabbed his wrist and bent it backward till he heard a loud crack. The demon screamed in pain and moved slightly away from John. Throwing a punch, his fist connected with the demon's face. Blood trickled from the corner of his mouth. *Well done,* he thought. John landed a round kick against the abdomen of the demon. He saw the demon panting, barreling over in defeat, but the demon still stood on his feet. *Damnit,* he thought. *This son of a bitch is still standing.* The demon did not move, so he retrieved the blade, grabbed the demon by the hair, and made him look at the blade up close and personal.

"How did you get that blade? Only certain demons have a blade like that. Did you kill one of my brothers, hunter?"

John shook his head. As he showed the blade's symbols to the demon, his other hand pushed down on the demon's shoulder. Using all his strength to prevent the demon from retreating or taking another blow toward him, he angled the blade so that the demon could read the words on the hilt. The hilt didn't just display the symbols of Hell, but it read, 'Asmodeus.' The demon froze in his spot and just stared at John.

"You are the heir to Asmodeus AND the demon hunter? Asteroth will not like this."

Before the demon could retreat, he said, "A patre meo." Then he plunged the blade into the demon, whispering the words, "Redire ad infernum."

To make his kill sweeter than it already was, John blew him a kiss before sending him back to Hell. Killing demons gave John a purpose in the world and a chance to repent for leaving the monastery. The demon was gone, but the defenseless human he inhabited was not. Leaving the alley, he double-checked to make sure no one saw him. As he started walking, pulling his collar up around his neck, he dialed 911 for the body left behind. After a few blocks, his cell phone rang. He answered.

"This is John."

The caller had a Scottish accent. "My name is Margaret. Were you once called Brother John a long time ago?"

John dropped the phone in shock, as he hadn't heard that name in centuries. It didn't break, but the screen cracked. He told the caller to hang on. He picked up his cell phone, shook off any dirt from the sidewalk, and placed it by his ear. "How did you get this number? Aye, I was Brother John, an exceptionally long time ago. I am no longer that person."

"I arrived in Los Angeles in search of Brother John. The organization I work for needs you. There is no other person with your unique skill set for our services. Meet me at the corner of Sunset and La Brea in three hours. I will explain everything, including answers you may or may not have received since your time in the monastery."

"I will meet you, but I make no promises. I will hear you out, but that is all I will promise."

He disconnected as fast as he could. It confused him how she'd found him since he always made sure he could never be tracked. However, she was right. He didn't have all the answers he sought a long time ago. The child had never revealed the truth over the centuries. It was infuriating to know he'd come close to killing the child, his so-called brother, many times.

Turning the corner, he figured he had time for a drink at the local bar since the meeting place was just a short walk away. He could get a look at her before they met. Sully needed sleep after the demon fight, but he promised to meet this stranger and hear her out. Maybe after.

He sat in the darkest corner of the bar and asked the bartender to keep the gin coming. Tonight's poison was gin, so he would still be on top of his game, no matter how many drinks he pounded. Gin and whiskey were the two liquors that never gave him a headache. He believed he owed that to his adopted father in Scotland. His father was always giving him sips of either gin or whiskey as a young boy. As he thought about that, a small smile crossed his face at the memories. So much that the bartender noticed. The bartender smiled and left him the entire bottle, saying that she expected the night to be busy since the other bartender hadn't shown up for his shift yet.

"Busy night?" he asked in his most flirty but curious voice.

"Yeah. My friend isn't here and I'm filling in again.

Second night in a row. The strange part is that he's been here all week. And he didn't even look sick. Now I work his shift and mine in this hellhole. Keep the bottle. It's on the house. You look like you need a pick-me-up. If you want something stronger, just holler."

The bartender turned on her heels and John got a good look at her. Her short hair made her look like a pixie with her small frame and that silver lip ring gave her a gothic look, but those pants on her made him stand at attention. While he'd honored his vow after all these centuries, he was still a man. The black leather also made him notice her more. She was a goth chick and someone to which he was attracted. He eyed her up and down while she served other patrons. She was not like the usual women that flirted with him with no success.

"Just checking on you, honey. Need something else?"

Holding up his glass in thanks, he nodded as she stared back at him. Although he wanted to press her more about her missing bartender, he saw other patrons required something of her first. He just kept pouring and watching the crowd get larger and larger. She had a minute to talk with him.

"You doing ok with that gin or need something stronger? I'm Mick, by the way. I don't recognize you, though. You're a new one here. This place can be a dump, but we've got the best drinks in town and cheap."

"I'm John Sullivan. You can call me Sully, though. It's a nickname that just stuck. Tell me about your friend. The other bartender. I can help."

"You like a cop or something? Private Investigator? Why would you want to help me? It's not like I have money. Look at this place. It's not even a club. I can't afford to pay you. Plus, he was just a coworker. It's just weird because he never missed a shift. We would always cover for each other. He would never just ditch a shift. Got a customer. Stay there."

***

Mick tended to the customer, but while she did, she kept stealing glances at the stranger. He had those smoldering eyes and something inside kept nudging at her. She had experienced nothing like that before. Before heading back towards the stranger, Mick never felt attracted to men. She avoided them because of her younger years. She'd grown up in the foster system, changing homes and never getting close to anyone. But at night, she would dream of Heaven and the beautiful angels. She always loved the stories of the archangel Michael. The wave of dizziness hit her like a ton of bricks and the hairs on her arm stood up and a wave of nausea made her lose balance. Her hand caught the side of the bar.

"You must think I'm a weird chick or something. I promise you I'm not. I just got lightheaded, you know?"

Sully smiled at her and a force seemed to pull her closer to him. Then she saw it. His aura. It was black and gold, something very unusual. She felt comfortable with him for unknown reasons. She told the stranger everything she knew. Mick described her friend as someone she could trust, especially during the closing shift when customers would get obnoxious. She wanted to know more about Sully. Mick gave a slight giggle at the thought of a nickname for him. Sully the Stranger. Then she caught a smile from him.

"I hope you can find him. But I feel like I know you. Are you certain you've never been here? You just have that face."

Sully said to her, "No. I am a stranger."

Mick chanced it. "You mean like Sully the Stranger? That's the nickname I'm giving you for now. It fits you, in a way."

She even laughed to show him she was playing with him. She smiled at him and filled him in as much as possible on her missing friend, hoping he would say yes to tracking him down. While she did, she noticed that his body was lean but muscular.

There was something that kept pulling her mind to thoughts of him. He was very handsome, even with his scars. The scars just made him sexier in her eyes. In fact, she wondered if she could bring him home with her tonight.

***

Sully thought about what she said. He'd never accepted money before, but he sensed that this could be something sinister. There was a smell in the room. The smell only someone like him would notice. The special gift made him different from others. He hated it. She sure was a pretty girl, though. He liked how she was wearing all black. Sully thought of people he knew. She was so beautiful. Intoxicating. She was not a demon, but she was human and something else. But he didn't know what.

He shook his head to clear his mind from such thoughts. But no matter how hard he tried, he kept thinking about how beautiful she was. Again, the aroma haunted him. There were demons here. He looked over his shoulder and all around the room.

Then he found him. Sitting in the back corner, alone but staring straight at him. His hat covered most of his face, but he was watching him and even glanced toward Mick. The trench coat covered the seat, but the demon moved a little, exposing a weapon. Sully wasn't about to let the demon live. It wasn't in his nature. He pushed his chair out, making his way to the demon, and sat down. Since it was a booth, both could hide their weapons under the table, but Sully wasn't about to hide anything.

"Demon."

"It's the little hunter. Where's your pet, hunter?"

Sully laughed and played along, but only to a point. He showed the blade to the demon and exposed his side, where a new symbol was now displayed from his last kill. He pointed with one hand to the blade and then to his side.

"This represents your friend. Tell Asteroth to leave me the fuck alone. And whatever the bartender is in here, do not touch her either. She's off limits to your kind. Mick's a cute girl, the innocent human that she is. Feel me, friend?"

The demon smiled and said, "I'll be seeing you,

hunter." He vanished from the body.

Before Sully could respond, the person in front of him just stared at him, unaware of what just happened. He smiled at Sully and told him he was afraid he remembered nothing that was said and that he might be a little drunk. Sully suggested it was time for him to leave the bar and go home. The man agreed. Sully made his way back to his seat.

Mick returned and gave him her friend's address, and she even had a spare key to his apartment. She smiled and said anytime he came in here, whatever he wanted would always be free.

"Tell me more about your friend."

"He's been working here longer than me, so he trained me for this job. But as we worked, we became friends. I gave him the nickname 'Ace' because he's always loved the idea of flying a plane. He should've been a pilot or something, but life didn't deal him those cards. He's tall, dark, and handsome. The usual for a bartender—just kidding. We're friends and I just know something's wrong. I can't explain it. It's not like him to not text me or anything for more than a day. We're close. That's why I'd be grateful if you could find him."

Mick touched his hand, and he felt a small tingle inside his body. Sully felt like something made him come alive. He smiled and left her a tip. He had time to inspect the apartment. Flipping up the collar on his jacket, he crossed the street and walked north. He glanced at the address written on the piece of paper. John watched the street signs to make sure he was in the right direction till he found it. It was a dreary apartment building from the outside given the neighborhood, but once he entered, it looked different. Cleaner.

He glanced around his surroundings and saw the stairs. No elevator. Still a dumpy apartment, but he was just a bartender in a low-rated neighborhood bar. And if he gave out free drinks like his friend Mick did, there wouldn't be much income rolling in. Two by two, he began hitting the stairs. The fifth floor was where he headed. He made sure no one followed him. Using the key, he slid it into the knob till he heard the click.

By the looks of it, the apartment was empty. It was clean, and not disturbed, so this was unusual. He kept looking around. A Bible was laying on a desk by the window. Untouched. Never even read. He noticed the bedroom, and it looked untouched. Then he saw it, under the desk where the bible was laying.

Faint chalk marks outlined the symbol of protection. He kept walking through the apartment.

Sully noticed the artwork was scarce, but a shit ton of alcohol was in the kitchen. Typical bartender apartment, he guessed. He wandered a bit more through the bedroom. Then his nose caught the smell of demons. But it was all over the place. Straining his sense of smell, he tried to narrow in on the odor. He saw nothing staring at him, but he knew something was there. He looked at the floor and didn't see a single symbol. The symbol for protection was by the desk with the Bible. Strange.

Removing his blessed cross from around his neck, he kissed it once as he clung to it. Speaking in the ancient language known only to the demons and angels, he summoned someone he had not seen in about five hundred years. The child. His brother.

The child had changed little. He still looked the same. Mischievous, and he seemed happy to see John. He greeted the child with a cold, hard stare. The child must've realized he wasn't here by an open invitation and broke the silence.

"Sully, brother, it's been a long time since I left your side. You look well."

"Cut the shit. Tell me what happened here. It smells of demons. Where's the man that lives here? His friend is worried."

That's when the child gave him a knowing look and an eerie smile. "He's alive, just not here. That's all I can tell you. You know I crossed the lines of boundaries for you many times when you killed our kind. You are one of us, even though you refuse to admit it."

"Quit your games. I'm not in the mood. If you don't bring him to me or tell me what I need to know, I will do what I did to you before, when you wanted to play your games. I will bind you to me once more and you can watch me slaughter the demons and they will think again that you betray them. We can play my game, brother. I'm tired of playing your games. I did that when we left the monastery." Sully emphasized the word 'brother' with great facetiousness.

The child walked into the room, hesitating. He sent telepathic messages to Sully, which he blocked or tried to, anyway.

"You can't fight your true nature, brother. I have a

better agreement. Let me tag along on your little adventures, and I will bring your man back to you. What do you say?"

Sully wasn't buying it. He was stalling. But for what reason? He agreed, but there would be conditions at some point.

"Ok, you can tag along, but after my meeting in a little while. You can't come to that. Prepare him for what? If any demon or whatever fucked with him, they will answer to me. Got it?"

The child giggled. "Of course, brother. Father would be so pleased that we are reunited again. He still wants to meet you, brother. The demons want the man for something. I don't know more than that. I just have two names for you. That's all I can give you. Abaddon and Asteroth."

Sully felt a gut-wrenching pull that made his universe collapse. He'd already dealt with two of Asteroth's demons and now Abaddon. The destroyer. *What the fuck was going on?* He didn't have time for idiosyncrasies since he had to go meet the strange woman that called him out of the blue. It was time to head out and finish searching the apartment later.

CHAPTER 2

Margaret was waiting for him near the corner of Sunset and La Brea. She glanced at her watch, wondering if he was going to be late. She did tell him in three hours on the phone. Margaret looked through the manilla file folder that they had given to her. She had studied his picture so many times before that she was sure she could recognize him. Her order was firm on her mission. Find Brother John and give him the satchel.

Margaret could not open the satchel or know its contents until after it changed hands. All she knew was that she'd killed several demons and others on her transatlantic journey. She looked down at her watch again. He better get here soon. She was a very punctual person. He had five minutes to go.

Margaret realized he wouldn't know who she was, so she waved in his direction and gave a little whistle. She saw him wave at her and he jogged across the street to meet her. Inspecting him, she compared what she saw to his picture in the file. The same dark hair, the same build, and the facial features matched. In her line of work, she could never be sure when working with demons and humans, and now a demon hunter.

She'd been put through the most intensive of all trainings given that her uncle ran the organization. Discretion was paramount and with people like Brother John, deception was the tactic of choice. She was impressed by his file, his hunting, but the organization had needs for him. And that was to be kept confidential, per her uncle. As she saw him come closer, she closed the file and waited for him to approach.

Taking off her glove, she shook his hand, but once their hands touched, a slight jolt shook through her, and she pulled hers back. He must have felt the same thing because Sully had a startled reaction.

"Brother John? I'm Margaret O'Leary, a member of the twenty-fifth generation of the O'Leary Clan. My family has been one of the trusted caretakers of the monastery where you spent the earlier days of your..um..former life."

"Nice to meet you. I'm just John now. No robes, no nothing. Just a simple man making his way in this world. You can call me Sully. I prefer it. What do you want to discuss? I'm a little busy right now, but your phone call earlier caught my interest."

"Let's head over to my car. It's parked over there. I have something they instructed me to deliver to you."

They walked over to her parked car and once inside, Margaret turned the ignition on so that the car could cool down. Los Angeles was a humid city, and she wasn't quite used to the heat. She handed the folder over to him, followed by the satchel. The file was thick, but she knew that the most important parts would be looked at first. He looked through the file, but she noticed he hesitated. This was her chance to speak with him in more detail, in a quieter tone.

"My family goes back to the days of the monastery, even before then, as they tasked us with the responsibilities of the secret hall. That's the room where you were last known to be with the demon child before he disappeared." She caught his blank stare before she continued. "Don't give me that look. I am very aware of demons and angels in this world, among other creatures. The O'Leary clan were the guardians of that demon child until the monastery took him. We lost track of you until about one hundred years ago. If you continue to look through that file, you will see about the last twenty years of your activity and other bio data. Look. Ask questions."

He stopped flipping through the pages and looked in her direction. Before she could make a move, he held a blade to her nose. "Do you know where I'm from? Who I am? What the fuck kind of file is this?"

Margaret was silent. She didn't want to move in case that startled him, and the blade would cut deep. Gently, she raised one hand as if in a sign of surrender. Then she nodded. "I know only what was told to me and what I read from the books in the vault. A lot of it is still cryptic and unclear, a lot is based on assumptions about what my family thought. Open the satchel, please. While you look at the contents of the satchel, I will try to explain the best I can. Know this: I do not know what is in the satchel. That satchel has been closed for years. My family came upon the satchel about six decades ago in the monastery where you were all those years ago. The satchel was in a vault but was found by the abbot then. He just knew to call on us to retrieve it. Triggers your curiosity, doesn't it?"

She waited for him to open the satchel, and then she spoke.

"We know that your father, the man who raised you, is not your real father. They gave you to him one morning and his wife, your mother, promised to keep your arrival a secret." She continued to watch him look through the satchel, but he did not pull any of the contents out. So, she continued.

"Your father, Benjamin Sullivan, raised you under my family's guidance. My family has been around for many generations, even before you were born. We are what the Holy Church, monasteries, and other religious institutions like to call sacred watchers. Since the beginning, angels and humans have produced children called The Nephilim. Demons and humans have produced children called The Cambion. You, however, are a unique matter because no one has ever come across someone like you. As far as the Holy Church is concerned, someone like you shouldn't be allowed to live, but we have petitioned them to convince you to help us, and in return, them. That you aren't on the other side. You are not born from a demon and a human or an angel and a human. You are something unheard of and we are still learning what that is. But our organization is important – we seek to protect humanity while keeping the idea that angels and demons walk among us secret. Humans aren't ready for that. Sure, they love movies with demons, angels, zombies, and others, for example, but that doesn't mean they are ready to share their living space with them."

She looked at him to see if anything registered, but all she got in return was a confused look and a long, hard stare. She wanted to comfort him, so she placed her right hand on his left, hoping he would not feel alone. Touching his hand shocked her, but she didn't let that show. Margaret noticed his scars and imagined him in the different demon hunts that had made him widely known in her uncle's organization as a formidable opponent. Her study of him also told her he was patient, kind, humble, and a man of deep convictions. It would not be easy to deceive him, but she knew she could. Knowing that he honored his vow to the Church all these years gave her the freedom to practice other tactics on him.

"What are you saying? I've lived for centuries and had this child with me for several of them, listening to his tales about my father. A father I never met, just heard of through him. The parents that raised me, well, they've been dead a long time. Look, lady, Margaret, or whatever you are, I don't enjoy games like this. I know what a damn demon is. I fight them. They come after me. It's like a marriage to me. I attract, hunt, and kill them. As far as my past, unless you can tell me what these things are in the satchel, there is nothing left to talk about."

Margaret, not wanting to fail her first mission and something she'd rather not divulge to the man sitting across from her, bowed her head and took back her hand. Margaret kept her true purpose of wanting to find him a secret. "Show me and I will see if I am familiar with them."

***

Sully pulled out the first item. Margaret looked at it. It was a faded piece of paper, like a parchment that Sully had used in a previous life. On it bore the symbols of the angels. Margaret took the parchment and retrieved a notebook from her purse. Sully noticed she started flipping through the pages as if she was trying to find matching symbols in her notebook. He slowly changed positions so that he could get a better look. Margaret kept thumbing through the pages, so he opened the conversation a little more.

"I have never heard of your organization before, even from my days at the monastery."

Margaret did not respond but kept thumbing through the pages till she pointed at something, turning the notebook to show him. "These are from the Enochian language. Language of the angels, the holiest language of all. Show me the next item please. Give me a chance to help you understand. I can help you, Sully."

Sully pulled out the second item. Another parchment piece, but with different symbols. As he handed it to her, he caught a small faint tint of what looked like blood on it, but from when and from whom was it? He had the 'gift' of smelling demons and the blood smelled demon to him. This sparked his curiosity even further. Closing his eyes, he inhaled deeply, hoping that she wouldn't notice, and he knew that smell. He just couldn't remember from what demon.

Margaret broke his silence. "It looks like this is from the Enochian language, but my notes show that it's a more demonic-like language. I can assume that this would be a demonic language. Keep going. Sully, are you ok?"

Sully nodded in silence to her question, but he didn't offer any sign of distress. Sully didn't have a good feeling about her, but she was the closest thing he came across in an exceedingly long time with knowledge of his history. He gave her the next few objects—a knife or blade, a ring, and a strange amulet. He saw Margaret reach into her purse and remove some tickets. She told him that each ticket had their names on it. As she handed him a ticket, that's when he realized she was bringing him home to Scotland. The rock in his stomach just got heavier. He was not comfortable with the situation, but he let it play out more. After all these centuries, he would find his answers.

"I'm not sure what else I can tell you about these objects. Is there anything else in the satchel? This is like a puzzle and, well, I've never been too fond of those things."

He offered her the satchel and she took it to look

inside. There was nothing else. But then she looked at the knife. He thought she looked at it with some familiarity, but he could be wrong. This was no ordinary knife. She opened the knife to examine the blade. It was an angel blade. Each angel has a blade like this to protect themselves from demons, Nephilim children, and many other things. But as she touched the blade, Sully got another strange feeling. It was like the blade was speaking to him.

"Ouch! The blade is sharp. Sully, take this blade and see if you recognize it."

He took the blade from her. Then she looked at the ring next. The head of a goat was on it and the stone was pure black. Sign of the demons. Sully watched her examining the ring. He knew the rings, as this was part of his mission. Know his demons. This was the ring of Asmodeus, an archdemon who served under Satan himself. Sully remained silent. But then again, he had never been a loud person.

***

She was having doubts about her purpose, but her instructions were clear. And she'd trained for this hour in time. She watched Sully's reactions and realized that he was more lost now than he might ever have been in his life.

"I take it that in the time spent with the child, it did not mention these things, did it? I know you have many questions because I would. There are two plane tickets. One for each of us. To take us back home to

Scotland, it seems. But they are open-ended. No date on them. I suppose I should tell you a little more about my purpose in finding you. I know little about your history or who your parents were. That seems to be a guarded secret, but someone trained me to assist you in finding the truth that you have always wanted as well as to support you in the choice that you will need to make. You wouldn't be a prisoner, but the answers might be in my family estate, close to the monastery where you served. It is still standing, you know. Say something. Please, this silence is killing me. My family has need of your exclusive services."

Sully still did not say a word to her. Instead, he got out of the car, leaving the satchel and all its contents behind, but she noticed he took the file on him. She left him alone for a bit as she waited in the car. Margaret continued to watch as he disappeared into the dark of the street.

"Damnit, Margaret!" She always mumbled to herself when things did not go exactly as planned. She waited hours for him to return. He did not. Then she found a hotel and checked in. As she sat alone in the hotel room, her phone rang. It was her uncle. Exasperated with herself and what happened tonight, she was abrupt with her uncle.

"How did the meeting go, Margaret? We are most eager to hear when he will join us."

Margaret inhaled. Then exhaled. "Uncle, I have a plan and it will require my patience. And yours. About Brother John. He goes by the name John now. Sully is his nickname, but only if he lets you call him that. He's not entirely sure about who he is. I don't think he realizes he is the one that the agreement is about. No one has ever told him the truth. And the satchel. That was strange. I will send you my report about tonight's meeting in a few hours. There is something different about him, though, and I will discover it."

"Just remember, niece, we need him here. The ancient text speaks about the passage, and he has to be the protector. He must be. This man fit all the signs. Keep me updated, niece. Oh, and your father sends his love."

The line went dead, and Margaret knew better than to ring him back. She took a hot shower and then sent her report to her uncle before going to bed. While she slept, she had the strangest dreams of Sully, but the dreams caused her to wake up flushed and unsatisfied. All she thought about was his body.

CHAPTER 3

Sully called Margaret late into the night. He didn't want to be rude but got straight to the point. "I need to find a young bartender before anything else. When do I have to decide?"

Her groggy voice told him he must've woken her up. She had offered to help him but he declined. She wasn't letting up on the issue because she wanted an answer for her family, and she hadn't planned on staying more than a few days. He agreed to her offer and said that he would meet with her tomorrow. He wondered how much sleep he would get tonight, if any at all. He stopped at Mick's place to see if she was working.

He walked into the bar and noticed the drunken crowd becoming volatile toward everyone. Sully saw Mick pouring drinks while a barback was filling the ice tub. He shouted to her, so she'd know he was there. She waved at him and smiled. "Gin or something stronger this time?"

Sully asked for one quick drink and told her he was going to look for her friend right after. It might take him some time, but he would find him. She reached as much as she could over the bar and hugged his neck tight. He threw back the shot of gin, smiled, and left her another generous tip. There was that smell. This time, the smell was from her. What was she?

"I'll be in touch, but I will need your number in case I need to reach you. I'll have someone to assist me, but I need you to stay away from his place completely. Understand? And no cops."

Mick gave him her number and two free drinks instead of one. Sully nodded thanks, finishing the drinks quickly. As he left the bar, her smell lingered in his nose. Thoughts went to her lips, her hands, and that sweet-sounding voice. His mind kept thinking many thoughts. He tried to rid himself of the thoughts.

Sully wandered back to his apartment and didn't lock the door behind him. His apartment was small but clean. The walls were covered with symbols that manifested themselves in his head, usually after a demon hunt. He painted the symbols on the walls in each place he lived. With the help of the child, he had tried to become familiar with the demonic symbols, but this one, what did she call it? The angel language. How would he know the angels' language? He understood little of what he was told. Sully knew he attracted demons, humans, everyone.

Deciding that this was too much for his head before it would implode on him in a massive migraine, Sully discarded his shirt and pants, leaving them on the floor. He needed a hot—a boiling hot shower to clear his mind. Walking towards the bathroom, he eventually discarded his boxers, only to find a guest waiting for him.

"Damn it, what are you doing here?"

The child just smiled. "You said I could tag along. Learn anything interesting?"

Sully ignored him. The child had never told him his name after centuries of knowing him. He should name the demon child already. The child looked at something behind Sully. Sully looked at him with curiosity. Then he felt it and then smelled it. There was something behind him. And of course, with no pants on, he didn't have his lucky blade that he kept hidden in his pocket. He had nothing to defend himself with but his quick wit and sheer strength. So, he casually turned around. Then he saw the other demon.

He recognized her, especially with those illuminating black eyes. The assassin of Lucifer, one of the seven kings of Hell. She lunged at him, instigating a fight, but he had no weapons. Just his hands. Oh well. As she lunged at him with a knife, his hand reached for her left wrist and clasped it. Using his left hand, he curled his fist and punched her in the stomach, hoping that the blow would dislodge the weapon she carried. It didn't.

Still holding onto her wrist, he tried to twist her arm. It must've caught her by surprise because she snarled at him. His feet moved along to hers, balancing them. Then his leg swept hers and she fell backward, losing the knife. Standing over her naked, he reached down and placed his hand on her forehead. Mumbling the words he used over and over during times like this, she vanished, leaving only black ash and dust behind. He'd sent her back to Hell, but she wasn't dead. John could never kill these assassins. *But why were they after him more now than ever?*

The child came out of the bathroom and saw the mess the other demon had left. "Smell that?"

Sully knelt on his knees, over the ash, and breathed in. He smelled nothing at first. He breathed in once more. Then he smelled it. He remembered this smell. He had smelled nothing like this since the monastery. It was familiar, but why? The smell was just not her smell, or any other demon smell he was familiar with.

He looked at the child and said, "I'm taking a shower. When I'm done, you and I are going to talk and this talk is long overdue, brother. You didn't give me answers hundreds of years ago, but you will tonight. And we are going to give you a name. Then I'm going to sleep if I can."

Sully took a long shower. As the steam filled the bathroom, he placed his hands against the wall, letting the water drip over his shoulders and run down his back. As he hung his head, he could see the various scars on his torso from all the fights he's been in. Each mark represented the death of a demon. Sometimes he fought angels, but he never killed one. He couldn't. That didn't mean they didn't want to kill him.

He just didn't belong anymore, as a monk or anything other. The hot water continued to run down his back, causing the steam to get to his head. He had never gotten lightheaded before. For the first time, he hallucinated, even though he wasn't faint. He couldn't tell anymore. It'd been one heck of a day so far.

His mind showed him images. Flashbacks of Scotland. Flashbacks of a baby being handed to a man. It looked like his father. And there was a handshake, and they gave his father something besides the baby. He couldn't make out what. The water had turned cold and brought him back to reality. He shook his head under the cold water. He must be tired. Turning off the shower, he reached for a towel and wrapped it around his waist. Using his hand, he made circles in the mirror to clear the steam.

His blue eyes stared back at him. Scars marked his face, but that didn't deter his good looks. Women still threw themselves at him, but he was reluctant. It was all about his promise when he entered the monastery. He couldn't keep his vow of silence when he faced the demons each time, but the monastery overlooked that piece because of the service required from him. But he would never break this one promise he could keep.

Sully had promised God a life of celibacy and he intended to honor that no matter how long he lived. He kept his hair short, and it was black as night, his body lean and muscular. He always wore his crucifix, and this was something his mother—well, adopted mother—had given to him when he was a small boy in secret. His father didn't know he had it. It would be valuable and rare today, given its age, but he let no one see it. He stared at his body covered with tattoos, protection symbols, and markings of being a demon hunter. He donned a clean pair of boxers.

He went into the kitchen to make a drink and offered the child a drink.

"You need a name unless you want to tell me your real name."

"You know I will never tell you my real name. That would give you power over me, and I will not do that. But I want to help you, brother. How about the name Peter, Paul, or maybe Matthew? Kind of fitting, is it not?"

That comment disgusted Sully. "Not any of those blessed names. How dare you! I will name you. You will be Edward. That will work."

The child gave him a look of defiance, but Sully stood firm. "It will be Edward, or I will banish you. I know how to, don't think I don't. I would've done it years ago, but you still hold the answers I want and need. You just won't give them to me. And I'm not interested in meeting my, er, biological father."

The child sulked until he finally gave in. At last, he could get some peace. But he still needed to find Mick's friend, and he had to deal with Margaret. First, sleep was demanding his attention. He gave in.

CHAPTER 4

Margaret waited in her hotel room for him to call. Having ordered room service and finished lunch, she didn't want to miss her mark. She figured if she didn't get too personal with him, the better. Better to call him her mark than address him as John or Sully, as he preferred. The more she thought about him, the more intense she was feeling toward him. Margaret didn't understand how or why—he wasn't only good-looking, there was just something about him that was alluring, including his smell, the way he walked, and his eyes. He had a certain charisma about him, and he was very attractive on the eyes. Her phone vibrated in her pocket, bringing her back to reality.

"Margaret, I'm sorry I didn't call back. Things just got busy for me, and I needed to digest what you shared with me. I'm not sure how I feel about all this. I've lived a solitary life and that's how I keep things."

"It's ok. I found a hotel and settled in. Do you want to meet today or anything?"

"I have something I need to do before I can think about the satchel and the file folder. Would you like to help me? I need to find a missing bartender."

Margaret was silent for a few moments. Then she gave him an answer after making him wait. Another one of her strategies.

"I would love to help you and in return, I ask that you give our discussion fair consideration before you tell me your answer. I know this is a world not known to many, but at least give it a fair thought. Sometimes it's just nice knowing there's someone out there who understands your unique lifestyle."

Sully agreed and then provided her with his address. He asked that she arrive soon so that they could get started and he mentioned he would have a guest as well. Agreeing to it, she hung up the phone once she confirmed his address after copying it down. She showered and then placed the international call, knowing her family had been waiting to hear from her.

"Da, it's Margaret. I've located him. He is the one, though he seems in denial about who he is. I know what to do. He doesn't realize who his mam is, but he won't acknowledge the demon within him. Do you have any updates for me on his file? I'm going to his address and see what I can discover. I gave the satchel to him, though he didn't accept all the information I presented. Tell Uncle that this will be done, and I am in full service to the organization. Once I get him on the plane, we will return, and the rest of the plan can begin. I will be in touch."

Margaret hung up the phone and prepared to leave. She placed her gun in the messenger bag, the extra ammo, and she retrieved her favorite knife from its compartment in her suitcase and slid it into her boot. She was ready for anything at this point.

***

Sully hung up the phone and turned towards Edward. "Okay, Edward. I have another person coming and she knows our history. She's going to help me with my immediate task, and you wanted to tag along. No interfering, deal?"

The child looked at him with solemn eyes but nodded in agreement. Sully tidied up the apartment and then pulled some of his useful weapons from the closet and threw them in his bag. Placing the bag by the door, he was ready. He and Edward still needed to talk.

"Edward, that ash smell – remember it? Do you remember the last time we smelled something like that together? It was a long time ago. Back there. In the monastery."

Edward just looked at him, as if he didn't want to answer. Sully was getting frustrated with him, so he kept prodding. Edward answered. "The scent is from the demons that serve Belphegor, one of the other Kings of

Hell. Belphegor sends his demons out when he wants something. He's aware of your existence. It's you he wants. It was more than Lucifer's smell or his assassins."

"Shit. What the hell is this, a feeding frenzy on Sully? First, Asteroth. Then Abaddon. Now Belphegor. What the fuck is happening in Hell? I'd send you back there, but you'd just enjoy it. *Brother.*"

Edward laughed. "What do you want to know, brother? You never call me brother unless you want something."

Sully grimaced before he answered. "All these centuries together, you still haven't told me the truth – the *entire* truth – about me or why you are always with me? You disappeared for a long time and then you came back. Are you going to stick with me or disappear without telling me what I need to know?"

"I told you all that I may tell you. The rest, our father said, was for you to discover when you were ready. But I'm here to stay. I left all those years ago because there were problems in Hell, and I had to be with our father. You need me now and he commanded I stay with you. To help you. To help you become ready to accept all that you will discover in time."

Sully mumbled something inaudible and slammed his fist against the wall. He looked at the key that Mick had given him—the one to the bartender's apartment. It looked like a normal key, but he sensed something off about it. Then he picked up the file folder on his "supposed" history. He looked through that with more diligence while waiting for Margaret. He opened the folder and looked at the first sheet. Standard Bio. Statistics. It was like reading his story from the past. Adopted child, raised by the kindest parents, but a simple farm life. Entered the monastery at age thirteen, a year younger than the age they accepted back then.

He realized that some of these facts were not accurate, giving him a sense of relief when it came to his history being made known to strangers. Parents killed in an unknown manner. Thinking about his parents brought him to tears. He noticed the child had said nothing in quite some time and when he glanced up, he was gone. Sully hated when he did that, especially when he just said he was here to stay.

He continued through the folder. It was pages and pages of history. His comings and goings, demons he had killed. The demons even had a bio on them. He flipped forward through the pages, and it was hitting him hard. There wasn't anything new on his life story that he didn't already know until the last page. Then he saw it. It hit him like a ton of bricks.

ASSUMPTION: 98% accurate
Biological Mother: ARCHANGEL

He dropped the file as the knock on the door startled him. It must be Margaret. He quickly put the contents of the file back together while yelling that he was coming to the door. He let Margaret in and just as he closed the door, Margaret handed him the satchel from yesterday. Sully's heart felt even heavier after reading the file. He took the satchel and sat down at the table. Sully forgot his manners and offered nothing to Margaret, but she didn't seem to mind.

"Sully, you look like hell. Have you eaten? Let me fix you something."

She opened the cabinets, peered in the refrigerator, and then said, "There's nothing in here that's worth human consumption. Let me buy you breakfast, a late lunch, even."

Sully shook his head and told her to have a seat. He planned to fill her in on the missing bartender. As he finished telling her everything he knew up to this point, which was not much, Edward appeared. He must've given Margaret quite the shock because she screamed.

"You...you...you're the..." and that's all that came out before she fainted.

"Just great, Edward. First, you disappear and then you scare Margaret to death. Great job, kid."

"Brother, we need to talk. It's not looking good for your missing man. Or for you."

Sully lost his patience. "If you are serious about telling me where he is, I will listen. Otherwise, shut the hell up."

Edward sat down and said, "Don't say I didn't warn you."

Before he could help Margaret, the door busted open and in walked three large men. Sully could smell them. Demons. With weapons. Sully leapt over the counter, yelling, "Oh, fuck." He reached one closet in the living room and pulled out his tricks of the trade. Vials of holy water. Then he reached into his back pocket and pulled out the blade he'd tucked in there earlier.

After several rounds of being knocked around, Edward jumped in next to him. Compared to his height, Edward was small. But that didn't stop him from touching one demon and destroying him. Sully didn't see how he did it because the surprise occupied him with the other two, who decided that two on one was more than fair play. Sully dropped and rolled to sweep his leg under them, causing them to fall. Using his blade, he stabbed it into both, causing them to die.

"I see you still have father's blade. The gift I gave you."

"It comes in handy when needed. There's no sentimental value to this. I need to check on Margaret."

He found Margaret coming around, but she was going to have a large bump on her head from fainting. He poured her a glass of water.

"Margaret, Edward. Edward, Margaret. Introductions completed. Now, let's get to business and see what's now going on in my life that's causing me way too many issues. Let's start with Edward. What the hell do we need to talk about?"

Edward replied, "The demons are going to come after you more and more. Somehow, you pissed off the wrong demon and there's a bounty on your damn head at Balam's command. He never issued one before until you really pissed him off. The missing man you want to find—he's the bait to bring you to them. Brother, this is much more important than whatever *she* wants." Edward pointed to Margaret, which only caused Sully to give him a hard look.

"Sully, did you read your file? There's something you need to know. It's in there."

"Do you mean the last page? Who my birth mother was?"

This must've gotten Edward's attention because his ears sure perked up, which told Sully that after all these centuries, he didn't know who his mother was either. This must have been some guarded secret their father didn't share with anyone. And now, it seems like the cat was out of the bag.

"Yes, Sully. A delicately crafted and studied assumption, but after generations of research and study, we believe the assumption to be correct."

"Who is your mother, brother? I want to know. Father said nothing to me."

Sully told him no. That was something that he would never share with anyone if he could help it, at least not until there was proof. He saw the child reaching for the folder, but he snatched it just in time. Since he had a photographic memory and there was nothing else in the file he didn't already know, he took the file and set it to flames with a lighter.

"Edward, I need to find the bartender's friend. You will either help me or I will kill you and don't think I won't. I'm tired of your games. I've endured centuries of them all because you promised to tell me things I didn't know and, well, you know how that ended. And Margaret, if you cross me, you don't want to see how angry I can get."

With Margaret and Edward both quiet, Sully settled into the business at hand. Finding Mick's friend.

CHAPTER 5

Once again Sully found himself in the bartender's apartment, but this time he brought along his new "partners" and his go-to bag of arsenal. At least that's what he liked to call it, since most people didn't understand his tools of the trade. He asked Margaret if she knew anything about the symbol by the desk or what she could make of it. She followed him around the room. Edward was just touching everything and driving him nuts.

"Look, we need to find him. Edward, do you know where he is and how we can get him back?"

Edward laughed. "He's with one prince of Hell and his demons. They took him because he discovered something they wanted. And as a bonus, they set it up so you would become involved, and they can get to you too. He's the appetizer while you are the main course, in a way."

Disturbed by what he had just heard, he didn't want Edward to know that. He needed to be on the upside of all this. He'd learned little more about his past in the last seven hundred years since that day with Edward than he'd learned in the few minutes spent reading the file. This was not going his way at all. He pulled Margaret to the side and asked if she was ok with Edward and all things crazy. She reassured him that this was part of her training and her family's aim. He also wanted to make it clear to her not to get in his way. Somehow, he felt that there was something she wasn't telling him. He could sense when he could trust someone, and he wasn't getting that feeling. He kept his guard up.

Sully looked in his bag and pulled out a vial of a bright blue liquid. It was something he'd created when they were back in Scotland all those years ago, and Edward had taught him a few things about demons and their vulnerabilities. When used, it would show the events that took place in the room as long as there was a demonic presence involved.

Sully wasn't sure how many days it has been since the bartender's actual disappearance, so the vial might not work. He cautioned the others to step back. He sprinkled the contents throughout the living room, as he thought this was where the activity took place, considering the layout of the desk and the Bible. A few drops fell on the symbol and the outline of the symbol turned the same color as the contents of the vial. This was a good sign. He continued to empty the vial throughout the room and asked Margaret and Edward to step back even more.

"Now we wait. The liquid will tell us what we want to see."

Edward was not patient. "I'll be back later. This is no fun." He vanished.

Sully was not happy, but he was more concerned about the bartender and what it would show rather than Edward's cowardice. Turning to Margaret, he joined her as they waited.

"This is incredible. My training did not include this, but then again, I've always trained through books and lessons. Nothing like this. I must admit, you are my first assignment."

"Oh great. A demon child. A newbie academia person who knows my identity. And me, whoever or whatever the hell I am. We make a group, don't we?" Sully let out a laugh during this intense moment.

***

Margaret laughed, then Sully silenced her. It looked like the liquid was steaming. A cloud of smoke filled the room, but it was not thick. Just thick enough to see shadows and whatever it wanted to show. The smoke changed to form shadows. Margaret was in awe at the sorcery that Sully possessed. She watched him as he whispered some phrases, and the room changed. She would've coughed at inhaling smoke, but this was different. Because she didn't want to distract him, she just made mental notes of his power and knowledge. It was amazing to watch him in action and not just read the text on him.

She made note of his cunning, strength, and power. The more she watched him, she realized he might be the protector that the organization needed. Sully was quick thinking, humble, a quiet leader that might get demons and angels to work together to destroy the agreement that her organization was after.

***

Sully could see the room. The bartender was sitting at the desk. The Bible looked open. Behind him stood several demons. They must've come out of nowhere and from behind. He didn't recognize the figures as those he'd met before, but a smaller shadow formed. He strained his eyes to see it more clearly. Then he recognized it. Edward. The demon child. Damn him.

Squinting, he continued to watch. The smoke showed him how the bartender fought them but lost. They didn't bother with the Bible. They took him and disappeared because the door didn't open once. The smoke disappeared.

"That was incredible. What was that stuff, Sully?"

"Oh that? That's something I learned a long time ago. Did you see the smaller demon? That was Edward. He's a part of this. And we led him right here. Why is he involved and now wanting to see me? I don't like this. We now know for sure that demons took him. Did you see he was looking at the Bible? Let's check it out."

Touching the Bible with his right hand, he then made

the Sign of the Cross. Though he may not be a monk anymore, he never once wavered in his faith. He flipped through the pages and noticed nothing right away. He closed his eyes. Sully never knew how he could do certain things, he just could.

Letting his fingers guide him, he went through the pages until his hands stopped. His hands would not let him turn the page. Opening his eyes, he read the part that his fingers stopped at. Then he noticed it. He hadn't seen it before. The words were not words, not like the ones you would find in a Bible. The entire book was nothing more than a disguise for these pages — they had the same symbols as the parchment paper in the satchel. Handing the Bible to Margaret, he said, "Look at the words. Right there."

Margaret took the Bible from him, and then she studied it. She removed a strand of her hair from her face, and that's when Sully noticed the tattoo on the inside of her wrist. He didn't question her about it, but he would later. The tattoo was a black pentagram with a red upside-down crucifix in the center. Small, strange symbols were printed in the center of each triangle. He knew what the upside-down crucifix referred to but there are seven princes of hell, so why five symbols? This was going to be discussed later. Sully did not like surprises and little by little, she was having a few too many surprises.

"This is the language of the angels. But how could a bartender have a copy of an angel book? This is not just any part of the book. It talks about a child that should not have been born. This child… it says that it will be the end of both Heaven and Hell should he or she live or choose a side. That's all I'm able to understand from it. This book is not to be read by humans, but some of us know it and trained the few."

Sully was not liking this anymore. His wanting to find out his history, his truth, led to a bartender being attacked, Edward acting strange and he'd have to go back to Scotland. And now some child is involved.

"Margaret, when do the tickets say we need to leave for Scotland? Mind you, I'm reluctant to go, but I owe it to Mick to find her friend. I think the answers I need are there, but I hate the idea of going back."

"We can leave anytime. What about the child? You're not thinking about taking him with us, are you? I am not comfortable with him, it, whatever he is."

"He knows we would have seen him in the smoke. The liquid never lies. He's part of this, and I think I'm going to keep him close to find the man. We need to see Mick. With luck, she might be working."

He took back the Bible from her. Sully felt the edges of the cover. It was coarse, not like the way Bibles feel. Taking a knife, he made a cut in the cover. It looked like it was a cover for another cover. Peeling back a small amount of the cover, he saw that this was nothing more than a disguise. Sully continued to peel it back, revealing a silver cover with the same markings of the angel's language. He couldn't make out what it said, but he wanted to double-check a few more places around the apartment because humans do not have books like this. It was a beautiful book. It felt perfect in his hands and out of habit, he made the Sign of the Cross and kissed the book in reverence.

Sully wanted everything and anything related to demons or now angels in his possession from this apartment. After about thirty minutes of searching through every nook and cranny, Sully loaded up his bag with books, clippings, a notebook that the bartender must have been keeping notes in, among stones with symbols on it. He took everything that might be useful.

Then he locked the door to the apartment, and they headed to the bar.

He found Mick working behind the counter and waved to her. She placed her bar towel on the counter and joined them.

"Mick, this is Margaret. And vice versa."

"Did you find him? Anything? My boss is getting so worried that we hired another bartender so I can stop working day and night. I can at least sleep, but I'm worried about him."

"We discovered what happened to him," he started, not wanting to say anything that would sound crazy. "We found what looked like evidence of him being taken by the looks of the apartment. Margaret here thought it would be better to clean up since we are not involving the police, to give us time to find him. Look Mick, this isn't a simple case…"

Mick interrupted before he could continue. "I don't have any extra money to pay you. I guess I overdid it, huh?"

Sully placed a reassuring hand over hers. "Mick, what I was going to say was this: I'm seeing this through, but this case got more complicated. Meaning I'm going out of town to find him and bring him home. I don't know everywhere I will need to go, but you need to know that your friend was into something that caused some unwanted attention from certain people. They may have left town, but we have the trail, and we will follow it. I will find him. You have my number. I have yours. But you will have to hold on to the gin for me when I come back. Deal? I will bring him back to you. I promise."

Mick had tears running down her cheeks as she said, "Oh, thank you. Thank you, John."

"Call me Sully, remember?"

Mick smiled, and Sully said that it was time to go. They needed to stay on the trail, but she could call him anytime she needed to hear an update. She hugged him until he loosened her hands but reassured her one more time before they left. He breathed in her smell and that's when he noticed Margaret was looking at her. He shielded Mick more from Margaret to ensure her safety and motioned to Margaret that it was time to leave.

CHAPTER 6

About a week later, Margaret and Sully arrived at the airport to be met by Margaret's cohorts. Margaret made the introductions and Sully mumbled his pleasantries. He hated flying, but there was no other way to get to their destination. One thing that he double-checked with Margaret was the travel arrangements. How were they going to get his weapons through customs? Margaret explained that the family provided airline tickets, so it left a paper trail. They checked in at a certain location but never boarded that flight. But if anyone checked, they would see that they had checked in, assuming that they were on the flight. Sully wondered about the limits of her family and their 'organization.'

The larger man informed them that the flight was ready, and their luggage loaded, which left Sully even more confused but armed with his wallet full of credit cards and cash, he wasn't overly concerned at this point about luggage. He knew he could buy whatever he needed there. The duffle bag he carried was one that was irreplaceable.

Margaret said, "There should be a smaller person—a child — accompanying us. Hopefully, he will arrive discreetly, or he will enter another way. Did you inform my father and uncle that we will arrive as soon as possible? The file has been read and destroyed. Relay that please."

The men led Sully and Margaret through doors and eventually into a hidden area of the airport. In front of them stood a black jetliner, and Sully made his way up the stairs. Inside looked like something out of a science fiction magazine. Sully saw computers lined up against one wall, reclining seats towards the back.

"Lifestyles of the rich and famous, huh, Margaret?" Sully was kidding, but he noticed she smiled at that comment.

"Sully, take a seat. We will discuss more once we take off. You will find the restrooms, a bedroom, and seats in the back. The kitchen area is behind the cockpit. The men will join us. They are our guards—well, my guards since I do not possess your unique abilities."

Sully took a seat in the back of the plane, reclined back, and closed his eyes. He didn't remember even taking off. He just let the vibrations lull him to sleep. It was about midnight by the time he opened his eyes, thanks to a restless nap. He saw Margaret was in the other seat, sleeping, so he just closed his eyes once more and drifted back to sleep.

In his mind, images were racing back and forth as if they were trying to tell him something. An image of a demon, unlike any other he has seen before, appeared. Thick, brown, wavy hair that reached his shoulders, a muscular frame with a long torso, and he had protracted wings. The wings were black with hints of white, but able to collapse when needed. A straight nose, muscular face with a near-perfect smile. If he didn't know any better, he'd consider this demon to be the most handsome he's ever seen.

On his right pectoral muscle was a symbol of a goat's head or something similar. Next, he saw this demon holding a baby while another demon was trying to brand it or something. Sully shook himself awake because the images disturbed his sleep once more.

He got up to get a coffee, but one man interrupted his first sip. "Is it true? You really don't know who you are? Or what you are?"

"I'm John Sullivan. My friends call me Sully."

"Take my advice. Heed what I'm telling you. Trust no one. And I mean no one. That's all I can tell you. The rest you will figure out why in time. And don't tell them anything about yourself, whatever you do. You'll see when we land. It's not all that it seems to be, especially with her. She tells you only what you want to hear and not all may be the truth. And if you know better, keep that demon child close to you whenever he shows up. Your father will protect you. But don't trust any of them, including Margaret."

Sully thanked him and told him he would take that warning seriously, though he wasn't sure why. He made his way back to his seat and remained awake for the rest of the flight. He periodically watched Margaret sleep until she finally woke.

"Tell me what you truly know about my past, my history, please."

Margaret smiled and pulled out her tablet. It took her a few minutes, and then she handed it to Sully. "Everything we have is here. Read away."

Sully read the electronic file on him and noticed that it differed significantly from the paper file he had read earlier. This included his financial information, which was not much to begin with, the exact flight and date he arrived in the States and the date he became a citizen. It even listed the different countries he'd lived in and, during certain periods, the people he had met. The only thing not listed here was his sexual orientation. It included all his birthmarks, each scar, each tattoo, everything. This was enough to give him the chills.

"Why exactly do you have all this shit on me?"

Secretly, he had hoped to catch Margaret in a lie, but what he got in return only made things more complicated. She smiled at him and didn't say a word for minutes.

"Sometimes the world needs a little protection from the things that they don't understand. To do this, we sometimes use our agents to manage those individuals with unique gifts. Like you. We want to train you in our ways and send you out to protect the world against the forces they do not understand. My family commits to helping the Holy Church and others in these situations. Similar to what you used to do, but you'd be working for us and not the Church or for yourself. We have an army that you would 'lead' to protect the world. Experienced hunters like yourself. And all are familiar with demon exorcisms."

Sully was silent. He listened. In his mind, they wanted to use him the way the monastery used him before he left. To control him. He remained silent, allowing Margaret to continue.

"So, your missing bartender would fit along those lines, and we would use our resources, our databases, to send you out to bring him back. You would work for us. A mutually beneficial relationship, with, say, occasional perks," she said as she slid closer to him to touch him, to entice him. But it didn't.

He pushed her hand away. "I made a promise to God. I won't break that promise. Not for you, not for any woman. When God tells me he has released me from this promise, that will be different."

Margaret didn't seem overly pleased at the rejection, but she accepted it. Sully didn't care. Still trying to wrap his head around the concept of what she'd just said, he just continued to stare at the data, telling his life story. Furious at other details they had known, but he was the only one who should've known. He slammed his fist against the screen. It's only been a few hours into the flight and he was getting fidgety and agitated.

"I'm going up front."

He found the big man that approached him earlier. Loudly, he said, "Can you please show me what's in the galley? I haven't eaten in quite some time."

The man nodded and led the way into the galley.

Sully whispered to him. "What makes you say not to trust anyone? Why should I trust you any more than I should trust this crazy story of hers?"

The man seemed like he understood Sully's predicament. He glanced towards the back of the cabin, and nodded to Margaret as if to get approval to use the galley by showing her some items that would allow them to continue the conversation. Sully could see Margaret approving and the man said, "I just bought us time to talk. Let's make something to eat."

Sully helped him so that he could hear more. He asked him some pointed questions, all of which he answered. Then the man said more.

"Because I serve your real father. The prince of demons himself, Asmodeus. What your brother has told you about him is all true. He is your father; you are his heir. I walk between the world of the O'Leary's and your father's in order to keep the balance. It's not fun, but it's the price of loyalty to your father. The O'Leary's are not what they appear to be. Don't believe everything Margaret has told you. They are an organization that serves the Holy Church but also goes against it. The organization's focus is to rid the world of all angels and demons, all of us. It took eons but Lucifer finally understood that there must be a Heaven and a Hell for the mortal world to survive. He called forth his demon princes to unite Hell and keep humanity in check.

"We would all sleep better if you would stop killing our kind, as you are one of us, but that is for your father to deal with, not I. I just do his bidding. Now, hand me that bottle over there. We're supposed to be cooking."

Sully obliged. He wanted to hear more, so he asked the man to continue.

"Sully, right? I'm going to show you something and you tell me if you have the same thing somewhere on your body. We each have our mark, but never in the same location. But first, my name is Ipes, but here they just call me Malcolm. I don't get to tell my true name to just anyone, but you are the heir, so I can tell you. I am the demon who knows the past, present, and future. This is not my true nature, what you see before you. But I shed that long ago to be here by my master's command. What do you really know or what have you come to believe about your true nature? You are not human, after all. At least not a full human."

Malcolm showed him a marking that was hidden by his clothes, discreetly. It was the same mark that he had. Sully had assumed it was a birthmark. Now, he wasn't so sure. He recalled his vision of the baby. Sully also realized that Malcom must not know the assumption of who his actual mother was. He kept mum on that piece of information till he learned more.

"Malcolm, not much. You would have thought for the centuries I have lived, I would know more by now, but not so. The demon child began a path for me, but it was all full of games and untruths. Maybe it was true, and I didn't realize it. It's not like my adopted parents raised me this way. And the monks at the monastery trained me how to use my so-called skill. I had to sort of train myself with the help of Edward, the demon child, to learn what I could about who I am. I gave him that name. So, you must know Edward then?"

"Your father sent him to the monastery, hoping you would get to know him while the monks were teaching you, so that you might be curious who your father is. Did you see the ring that was in the satchel?"

"Yes, Margaret gave me back the satchel. It's in the duffle."

"Put the ring on. It is the ring of Asmodeus. The organization doesn't know how to use it, at least not yet, but it is your birthright. You are the heir. Asmodeus' heir, but they don't know that yet. They just think you are another demon hunter with gifts like no other. I know what they put in the satchel. Before handing it to Margaret, I carried the satchel. I know your file. Your father doesn't want demons to die by your hand, but you've been doing that for a long time, and he is not interfering. He has other plans for you instead. Back to the real story behind the organization. Let's see what else I can tell you. It's hard because I've served them for so long. They think I am a stray demon, with no loyalty to anyone but them. This organization primarily uses the Holy Church's name on face value but in reality, they want to destroy both Heaven and Hell. The rest you will learn in time. Most importantly, do not trust Margaret no matter how tempting she can be."

Sully was in disbelief. He'd heard of Asmodeus, one of the most powerful demons in the world, but did not realize that he was his father. Asmodeus was the king of all demons and if Edward, the child, is also his son, that truly made them brothers. Do they share the same mother? He realized he had more questions than before.

"Thanks, Malcolm. I don't trust anybody usually, so that will serve me well. What will happen to me if I wear this ring? Demons already know how to find me. I don't want to be their attraction magnet even more."

Malcolm laughed. "Take this bowl. I'll bring the plates. We will have time to talk more later. Wearing that ring will inform the demons who either serve Asmodeus or oppose him that you are his rightful heir. Those were my instructions from him. To tell you your father's name."

"I hate games."

Taking the bowl, he made his way to a table area where he and Malcolm sat. Malcolm pretended to eat while explaining to Sully all that he could. Sully began eating and over time, he forgot how hungry he was.

CHAPTER 7

After a long flight, they landed in Scotland and Margaret completed the hotel check-in. She noticed Sully looked extremely tired and suggested that he retire for the rest of the day. Margaret was also weary, but she knew she needed time to check in with her da and uncle. There was still much to do to secure Sully and his compliance.

Based on his behavior and attitude so far, she knew it was not a simple task to get him to comply to help the organization. She handed him the key to his room and said that her room was on a different floor. Margaret watched him turn around and head towards to elevator.

Taking out her secured phone, she pressed a number and waited for the connection. She had a direct line to her uncle since he actually ran the organization. As much as she loved her da, it was her uncle that she had to obey.

"It's me. We are in the hotel, but if you want him, you need to come quickly. He is tired and we may use that to our advantage because of the jetlag. I don't think he will come willingly, but I can try. It will just be faster to come get him now, unconscious, of course."

The voice on the other end responded.

"Aye, niece. I will send four men. Leave a message for me with the room number and the men will take it from there. They will come tomorrow, so head to your room and just wait. If you meet with Sully as I suspect you will, just tell him that the plan is that you will drive to headquarters. Once the men leave, head here for further instructions. It will impress your da with your service."

The line went dead.

Margaret followed her uncle's instructions and provided a generous amount of money for the concierge that, should there be questions, the organization has it handled. The concierge took the money and nodded. She knew that there would be no questions about what would happen when her uncle's men arrived and dragged an unconscious man out the door with the donation. Margaret headed to her room and decided to just take a quick rest, since there was no need to unpack. Her uncle had been clear. Tomorrow.

***

Sully made his way to the room. He met a hotel employee on his floor and the man offered to help him.

"Sir, let me help you in. Welcome to Scotland, sir."

"Thank you, but I'm rather jetlagged. I just need to rest."

"Of course, sir, but let me show you the room offerings."

Sully declined. He just wanted a solid, peaceful sleep with no distractions or images that would haunt him, from anything. The employee unfastened his cuff link and showed him a mark without saying a word. It was the same mark that Malcolm bore, that he bore. It was a mark showing allegiance to his demon father.

"Rest, sir. Acknowledge the path your birth has placed you on. I'm one of your father's demons, heir. If you need anything, here is my phone number to reach me and take this other phone to place the calls. I also suggest that you visit the lounge after you rest. You will find it most entertaining. But don't trust the woman you are with."

"What the hell is going on?"

The concierge smiled. "Miss O'Leary knows more than she wants to let you know. Be wary and I believe Ipes told you, do not trust them. Sleep, heir. Sleep."

He bowed and left Sully alone in the room to ponder what was going on. The demon child, Edward, never showed up on the plane, but somehow Sully already knew he would see him shortly. It was just a feeling he had. That's just the way things were between them. More than anything, he wanted to figure this out and get his life back. He worried about Mick and the missing bartender. Sully decided he could rest for a bit and then go to the lounge.

Hours later, he sat alone in the lounge. Sully hadn't seen Margaret but given everything he has learned in the past twenty-four hours, he wanted space. He brought his satchel with him, hoping that the privacy would allow him to get a feel for what was going on. Or at least maybe who he was.

He held the ring in his hands, as if waiting for it to tell him tidbits of his past. Instead, it just shone in the light. He wasn't ready to put it on, but as he held it in his fingers it felt natural to him. He laid it on the table. Next was the parchment with the symbols on it. Both pieces had symbols he wasn't fluent in, but he held on longer to the one that bore the Enochian language. He hoped it would speak to him or something. He couldn't get the thought out of his mind—a demon king for a father and an archangel for a mother. Sully wasn't sure what to make of it or if it was even possible. It challenged his upbringing in the monastery and his faith.

Lost in thought, he didn't see Edward sitting next to him or even when he came in. Edward seemed intrigued, looking at the items on the table. Sully noticed he was eyeing the ring but said nothing. He gathered the items and placed them back in the satchel. He wanted space except as soon as he got up, Margaret was entering the lounge.

"Oh great," he muttered.

Margaret eventually found her way to his table. He wasn't in the mood for any of this and all he kept focusing on was the bartender. That was most important to him. He hadn't known his parentage or his full history for centuries, so why should he care now?

"I didn't realize I'd find you here, Sully. We have a long drive ahead of us to the compound and we're only going to be here a short while."

"Look, Margaret, I appreciate you helping me with the missing bartender, but that is my only priority right now. I'm not interested in the compound or anything you must show me now."

Margaret looked confused but said nothing else. Her eyes glanced toward Edward and then back at Sully. Edward squirmed and nudged Sully on the shoulder.

"Sully, you and I need to talk about the bartender. I have news only for you."

Sully took the hint and said they would find Margaret later. But before they could leave, the bartender came to the table with drinks. Being polite, Sully said, "We will tend to that after we finish this drink, Edward. Margaret is our host, after all."

Edward shrugged and said, "I will meet you in your room. Give me your key, please."

Sully handed him the key and told him to be careful since they were guests in the hotel. A few minutes later, he was back in his hotel room talking to Edward.

"Brother, look at the pieces of parchment carefully. What do you see?"

Sully studied the pieces and he realized they fit together somehow. The jagged edges seemed to go together if he could line them up right. He looked throughout the room to find something to tape them together and when he did, he realized the symbols were not really symbols. They looked like symbols in the language but he couldn't be sure. His heart was beating faster upon this discovery. He looked at the satchel once again, this time with a closer eye.

The ring for once stood out to him, though Sully didn't understand why at this point. Having nothing to lose, he put the ring on. As it fit around his ring finger, it burned him. His finger wasn't turning red, but he could feel the intense fire within his skin. The ring stopped. It had sealed into his flesh somehow. The goat's head changed from just the outlined shape against the black stone to a crimson red. He tried something new. He held the parchment to the ring, allowing the crimson-red color to shine on the parchment, and there it was. The symbols changed to one word. JOPHIEL. As he mouthed the word, the word completely disappeared, and the pieces blew up in flames.

He couldn't be sure, but Edward might have seen the word. He had to know there could be trust, but after all this time, he didn't know if he had the strength to trust Edward.

"Did you see the word?" Sully asked.

"Yes, brother. But I know you don't trust me. I feel what you feel, remember?"

Sully hated that, but he knew he was right. And it would make sense, considering they were brothers. He was coming to terms with things after all this time. Might as well be a little more friendly to the demon child. He needed him because he was the only one who knew where the missing bartender may be.

"Edward—do you like that name or do you want a different one? And you can call me Sully from now on."

Edward took a few minutes and finally said that the name was ok. "But, Sully, what are we going to do about Margaret? I don't really like her."

"Yeah, they warned me about her. But I'm not focusing on that right now. Do you know what the word means? I know you saw it before it all went up in flames. If we are going to trust each other, now is the time, brother."

Edward shrugged. "Yes. I saw it. Now I know why Father is so protective of you. Your mother is not human. She's..she's an archangel."

Sully kept his calm at what Edward just said. Now was not the time to panic. "We must not let Margaret know what we know. Right now, everything remains as before. You and I need to check out a few things in this place. Can you help me find Malcolm?"

Edward nodded.

"And let's get things straight. Since we are going to have to trust each more than ever, call me Sully from this point on, and I will do my best to tell you what I can as long as you promise to do the same. I have a feeling we are going to be sticking together for some time."

Suddenly, Sully was not feeling well and before he completely collapsed, the door opened, and he saw four large goons approaching him. One had a hooded mask, and the others carried guns. Sully didn't even have a chance to sleep. Yet.

CHAPTER 8

Margaret's room phone rang, and it was the concierge from the front desk. She wasn't expecting his call.

"Miss, the men have picked up the message. They are on their way to the room. Your uncle also called the hotel and doubled what you gave me to call you. They instructed you to leave the hotel now."

He hung up on her.

Margaret couldn't make sense of this as it deviated from the instructions she'd received from her uncle not that long ago. Something gnawed at her, and she went to Sully's room. As she reached his room, she saw the door was open and there seemed to be a bit of activity coming from the room. Knowing that the bartender was supposed to drug his drink if he ever showed up at the lounge because she'd arranged it, there shouldn't be any resistance because the drug was slow acting.

As she appeared in the doorway, she saw Edward screaming and fighting some men. For a child-sized demon, she saw that Edward could really hold his own. Hanging onto the back of one of the men, Edward was punching away at the base of his head. Holding in a laugh, Margaret thought that the man was going to have one awful migraine after this. Sully appeared to be wounded, but he was not unconscious. How could that be?

Then she realized that these were not her uncle's men at all. She screamed at Sully to fight. "Sully, these are not my uncle's men. I do not know who they are. You need to fight them."

Once she said that she realized that she'd just given everything away. She knew Sully would not trust her now, and that he was a pawn. There was no turning back now.

***

Sully heard her voice, and something snapped. His adrenaline pumped, and the blood felt alive in his veins. Sully couldn't explain it, but there was something that was triggered inside and before he knew it, his vision somehow changed. For as long as he could remember, he'd had perfect vision. But this was something else. Through an aura, he saw the true nature of the men. These were demons he has never seen before. But they bore Lucifer's mark. More assassins from Lucifer. *Damnit!*

Sully let the adrenaline take over his body and his tattoos burned into his flesh, turning red. It took the sheer willpower to wait those seconds for everything to kick in. Three of the demons watched in horror as Sully leaped onto the biggest one and dug his nails into the sides of his head. Blood dripped from the sides of the man's head and that's when he realized that his fingers had grown some serious claws.

The demon screamed and in Latin, and Sully screamed something in his ear. The demon melted into a puddle once Sully let go of him, the claws retracting. Before anything else could happen, Sully charged after the other three. He took the crucifix from around his neck and whispered the prayer he always used to exorcise demons. The room was silent. Anyone looking at the room would immediately know a terrible fight took place here. Tables were knocked over, chairs were on the floor, and broken glass was everywhere.

Sully looked at Margaret and shook his head. "I heard you. Thank you for snapping me to attention but how could you? Who are you exactly? I need you to leave." He wasn't about to give Margaret a chance to say anything.

Margaret was upset. It showed on her face. "I wanted to help you. Let me help you. I can be a trusting ally if you would just let me."

Margaret was really trying hard to stay by even helping to clean up the room. Sully wasn't having any part of this game with her. He moved closer to where she was picking up a chair and abruptly said, "You need to leave.

Don't argue with me. You want me to trust you? Then leave. Show me I can trust you to do that at least."

After she left, he told Edward they were leaving the hotel.

***

It had been a few days since arriving in Scotland and Sully kept Margaret at a distance while he contemplated his next move. Taking to heart what Malcolm told him, he just didn't have a trusting bone in his body about anything anymore. Yet, he'd learned about the possibility of his parentage from Margaret and, well, he already knew a little about his father, but not the level of detail that Malcolm filled him in on.

But there was still the bartender to find. The missing bartender. *How the hell does he fit in with all this shit?*

"Edward, since we are here, how would you feel about visiting the old monastery? I know it's still standing but I just want us to pay our respects. What do you say?"

"Sully, brother, I'd rather not. I don't like that place. I remember what you did to me. But I will go if you must. None of the monks you know are even alive, so why should we bother?"

Sully put his hand around Edward although he was a demon, he still looked like a young child of about ten or twelve. Then he told Edward that they were going because perhaps, though the monks were not the same, the secrets within the monastery were. Edward gazed up at him and smiled.

Missing Bartender. Secrets. Son of a demon and maybe an archangel. The life he once knew was changing at a fast rate and, eventually, he had better come to terms with things. Hailing a private taxi, he provided the driver with the name of the monastery that they wanted to visit. He paid upfront. Sully had learned over his lifetime that if he paid a little extra for things, things always had a better way of working out for him. Edward leaned back in the seat and Sully wondered why, even though he was an older demon, he continued to possess the look of a young child. Maybe he thought it would be easier to blend in this way.

The driver made the usual small talk, and Sully obliged him. He needed to understand the changes in Scotland over the last seven hundred years, giving nothing away. As Edward slept, he learned more about the political climate, the social changes, and the people than any news article or book could've provided, especially about the monastery. Sully learned that a few months after they left that night, one of the previous monks was dead, hanging by his bedsheet. They found a note that his death was to be blamed on Brother John, but there was no Brother John to be found.

In fact, the abbot had gone on record saying that Brother John never existed and rumors in the village sparked interest in nearby towns about a mysterious monk named Brother John. The authorities found no trace of him, and the abbot forbade entry into the monastery since that dreadful event of the prior's death. Years later, there were rumors that the monastery was empty, as there were no signs of any monks continuing to live there. As the driver continued talking about it, he let Sully know that not all rumors are true because there is no other monastery around the area.

"You must be new to Scotland. I don't recall ever seeing you around before. And I've been driving for over twenty years now. It's how I met my late wife."

"Yes, sir. My young son and I are just traveling, and I wanted him to experience culture at an early while he can appreciate it before life gets too busy for him in the future, with maybe a career, family, you name it. I was, um, wondering where I could find more information about that monastery and the abbot. I've always been interested in history, especially that of monasteries and old churches everywhere. I would appreciate it. My name is Sully by the way."

The driver smiled in the rearview mirror. "Nice to meet you, Sully. My name is Michael Darby. I think the monastery's records are in the town hall, but honestly, I'm not sure how far they go back. This situation I was telling you about happened something like six or seven hundred years ago. I don't believe my family history even goes back that far. I'm sorry if maybe you thought it was recent. My English isn't always that good. My wife would always say that I will confuse people if I don't improve my English language," he said with a hint of laughter. Sully thought he must be remembering his wife, which is why his laugh sounded so sincere and fond of the memory. Not like how some people reacted after losing a spouse.

Sully nodded and mentioned his humble thanks to the driver. He didn't want to let too much information out about his personal knowledge of the monastery, so he sat back and was quiet for a short period. Then, he continued the most pleasant conversation he has had with another person since the night he met Mick. Sully noticed Edward had fallen asleep, and he just put his arm around his "son" to keep up the ruse in the private car.

After what seemed like an eternity, Sully opened his eyes and realized that he must've dozed off. The driver didn't wake him until they reached the gates of the monastery.

"Here's where I drop you off if you are sure you want to go inside. Should you want to visit the town hall, there is a footpath to the left of the monastery. Walk the path but know that it is only about fifty years old, so it should be easy to spot. Anyway, follow the path down to the center of town. Make a left by the fountain and keep going straight past a bakery. Oh, what was that bakery's name? Cuckatoo or Cuckoo or something like that. My mind is blank, as people say. Regardless, you can't miss that bakery. It has the most delicious cakes. The town hall is right past the bakery. You won't be able to miss it. Take my card. If you ever need me again for hire, I will come. It was a pleasure to meet you."

Sully took the card and woke Edward. "We're here, son."

Edward stirred, looked confused, and shrugged. "Ok."

Sully thanked the driver and said he was grateful to him, especially for the information, and he would be in touch. Sully and Edward waved to the driver as they watched him disappear down the road. Turning to look at the monastery, Sully felt a sudden sadness at the thought of his brothers from that fateful night when both he and Edward left, never to return. The abbot, the man that knew and trained him for his mission in that room, accused or worse, to know that his second committed suicide. He wondered about the others, minus the two that had died that night. As brothers, they made their way to the large doors of the monastery. Sully pulled the cord that hung to the right, and they could hear a loud ringing.

The door opened, and an elderly man looked at both Sully and Edward with a curious eye. He removed the whiteboard that hung around his neck and wrote a message, showing it to Sully.

I am the abbot of this monastery. We do not accept visitors. Go away but go with God in your heart.

Sully motioned to use the whiteboard to respond. In his message, he let the abbot know that he was interested in the monastery and was hoping to see inside if the monastery's old ways were intact. He wrote out two words: *sealgair deam*, and made sure that only the abbot's eyes saw them. He did not want Edward to give anything away.

The abbot looked at Sully, and then feverishly began writing on the whiteboard again.

It's been a VERY long time since we did that. We have no demon hunter here anymore. There are but only a few, especially those sacred to the order.

Sully nodded to show that he understood and responded in writing.

I am taking a risk by telling you this, but I can see you are no fool, abbot. The demon hunter of this monastery is me. They knew me as Brother John, precentor to the monastery, a very long time ago. I served under Abbot Alistair. Do you have records of my role as the sealgair deam, demon hunter?

The abbot looked at him with awe, but not with any confusion. Sully took this as a sign of good faith. The abbot invited them both in and made the motion for them to respect the quietness of the monastery. Sully followed the abbot through a series of familiar hallways and while doing so, he placed his hand on Edward's shoulder as if to reassure him that things would be ok. The abbot stopped in front of the door that Sully thought he would never see again.

CHAPTER 9

The door opened, and the abbot made the sign of the cross. Then he bowed his head as if in prayer, something Sully was very familiar with because he'd done the same thing on the last night he was here. Then the abbot turned to Sully and Edward and wrote on his tablet: *We can speak freely in this room only.* Sully turned to Edward and gave him a nod of encouragement.

The abbot broke the silence. "In this chamber, I became the one to fulfill the role you left behind. Though I am not as old as you, and our monastery had gone centuries without a hunter, I had my calling." The abbot coughed.

The abbot must not have used his voice in some time because of its raspy sound. He placed a hand on the abbot's back as a sign of comfort for him.

"I understand, Abbot. It takes a toll on our vows to the Lord above and our duty that must be in this room. It's like we serve two masters. The master and Lord of all that is good and the master of exorcising these demons. Please, take your time. I am simply a guest in your monastery, seeking your help if you will give it to me."

"Brother John, we have not used this room in many years. The last demon exorcised from here was over thirty years ago, and it was not a powerful demon. But, let me not digress. I am not a young man anymore. After you left that night, that's when the strangest things happened. The abbot's prior killed himself, blaming you, but the abbot destroyed the physical evidence. He had the monastery historian make recordings. One month later, another monk went insane and eventually killed himself after killing two more brothers. The abbot couldn't understand what was happening. It was gruesome, but we have the historical recordings in our library. The abbot denied everyone's assumption and accusation, even forbidding the monks from setting foot outside the walls again." He continued to cough, this time spewing a little blood.

Sully turned away from the abbot, but the abbot placed his hand on his shoulder, gently reminding him of his own abbot all those years ago. A tear fell from his eye.

"Brother John, no matter what name you go by in this life, you are still one of us. The abbot from your time did what he did to protect you, not to blame you. You are the chosen one of this monastery to rid the world of demons."

Sully asked the abbot about his cough, noticing the blood at the corner of his mouth. Taking a handkerchief from his pocket, he handed it to the abbot, who in turn nodded his thanks. The abbot told him of the demon that he had to exorcise from one of the brother monks because he was killing the monk from the inside out. As Sully listened, he noticed Edward clung to him as the abbot explained that night's terrible fate. It had not truly exorcised the demon. But according to the abbot, they needed it to calm the brother monks. The abbot continued to tell Sully that the demon lives inside him, feeding on him slowly. The abbot simply wasn't strong enough to rid himself of the demon.

Edward tugged at Sully until he knelt down, since he was a child's height. "Sully, brother, maybe you can rid him of this demon?"

Sully looked at Edward, and never in all these years was Edward keen on exorcising one of his own.

"Why this one, Edward? Don't tell me you are afraid of it?"

Edward gulped and shared his information with everyone in the room.

"The demon inside you, Abbot, is not one to take lightly. Listen carefully, this demon is a soul eater. It doesn't just eat your insides, it feeds on your soul, little by little, and at the last minute, it will emerge stronger than you and it will turn you into a demon. One of Satan's little surprises is that the princes of Hell don't like it. It helped keep the princes, like Asmodeus, our father, in line because these new demons are the pure vessels of Satan. It's not good. I look like a child but in my years, I am not, and I know when to be afraid. This is one of those times."

The abbot looked at Sully and he could feel his heart being torn between handling his business and helping the abbot. Time was not on his side if he wanted to stay eluding Margaret. He made a choice. The abbot. Finally, he asked the abbot to lie down in the center of the room and instructed Edward to draw a dark lined circle around the abbot with at least three feet between the line and the man. Edward created the circle that matched his directions.

Sully opened his bag, removed the crucifix from his neck and kissed it before placing it in a case in the bag. He didn't know how he was going to exorcise this demon, but he felt obligated to help the abbot and free him from this pain. Looking at the man lying there, he looked up to the ceiling as if to pray silently and then looked down at the ground, also as if asking for his father's strength. Something he had never done before.

Sprinkling holy water on the abbot, Sully said the prayers loudly, and then in a whisper, he called upon his father, Asmodeus. He wasn't sure about doing this, but he knew he needed power if the demon was truly one of Satan's vessels. Sully took another look at the abbot and noticed that his breathing was shallow. Then his breathing stopped. Sully was panicking inside but didn't let Edward see it.

Above the sound of a whisper, Sully called out to Asmodeus. "Father, be at my side now. I ask for your help against the soul eater and in return… in return…" he paused as he looked at the abbot. "I will commit myself to you, forsaking all vows made to God. You know I am your son. I give you my allegiance in return for this man's freedom from the soul eater. I swear upon the sacred parentage of my mother. And to you, my Lord, forgive me, for I do not know how else to save your beloved servant, the abbot." He hoped that would be enough to bring Asmodeus to the room from his place in Hell.

He sprinkled the holy water once more to ensure that the abbot received a blessing if he could not survive this. Then he felt it. A finger touching his shoulder and a newfound strength in his body. Sully turned around and saw a man that he closely resembled standing in front of him.

"Son."

"Father."

Well, shit. This was an awkward moment. Asmodeus raised a hand, and before Sully could react, he realized that his body was immobile. He couldn't move, he couldn't speak. But he could watch with his eyes. That's when he realized that Asmodeus controlled his body. He raised his own hand. Then he heard the voice of Asmodeus.

"Anima comedentis, hanc tibi licetiam trado. Redi cui servis. Obede nunc, vel revertere ad Dominum in gehenna."

As Asmodeus lowered his hand, Sully moved. Looking at the abbot, he saw no change. That demon inside was an infuriating son of a bitch. Rage filled him and somehow, he knew that this must be from his newfound allegiance to his father. He reached for his father's hand for strength, and as he held hands with his father, his voice became more commanding. He repeated the words his father said, louder and more powerfully.

This time, the body convulsed and writhed in the circle. The smell of burning flesh filled the room, along with the abbot's urine. The flesh was burning because it touched the rim of the circle. Sully saw Edward hide in a corner, afraid to be near the demon. Again, he repeated the words. This time louder than ever. He would not let the soul eater remain in the abbot for another minute. Finally, the soul eater emerged from the abbot's mouth. It stood in front of Sully but was still in the circle. The circle kept it bound inside.

"You seek to destroy me, the vessel of Satan? Asmodeus, you are not that powerful to have me withdraw, so who is this fool who demands my appearance?"

Sully had never faced a demon like this in all his years as a demon hunter. But this time was different. Fear did not faze him. It was as if part of him, the part that made him pure from his mother, was dying.

"I summoned you. Return to Hell, to your master, and leave the servant of God alone."

The soul eater laughed, and before Sully could react, the soul eater entered his body. He fell to the ground and called out for his father.

CHAPTER 10

Asmodeus was looking at Sully when his eyes opened.
He felt strange somehow. The demon that was staring
right back at him had his face, his body, but his eyes were
darker. The likeness was fathomable. Sully hoisted
himself on one elbow and noticed that Edward was also
at his side.

"I am Asmodeus, your father. Of all the impossible,
thick headed, imbecile things to do. You use your mother
as proof of your allegiance to me? Stupid piece of shit.
You don't do that to your mother. Do you even know
who she is? Spineless idiot."

"Now, father," Edward spoke. "You wanted me to
stay with him all these years and never has he used her as

a bargaining chip. The soul eater would have destroyed the abbot, and Sully would never let that happen. Remember, he is the son of you both. Well, dammit, now I am defending *her* and I didn't mean to."

Sully finally found the strength to stand up, still dizzy from the merge with the soul eater, but it was not his voice that came out when he spoke.

"Asmodeus, prince of demons. Give me this vessel for my pleasure. Let me consume him. His soul is not entirely of our kind, nor human. Wait… his existence is not that of a human mother, but something more powerful. You kept him a secret all these years. Why? Does not matter now. I serve Lucifer and it is he who will want to know of this immediately. Mind if I take him on a small trip?" Cackling hysterically, Sully watched as his father and brother stared back at him. He couldn't fight the control of the soul eater nor resist the hold that he had on him. All he could do was watch from the inside of his body as the soul eater took control of his body, his voice, his eyes.

Silently, in his mind, he tried to flee to a place deep in his being where the soul eater could not interrupt his thoughts. He kept running in his head, following twists and turns. His damn mind was a maze. But something made him stop right in his tracks. It was a shadowy figure, but he sensed it wasn't evil or malevolent. He just waited.

The figure raised a small finger in front of him and then extended it to what would be his right. Sully followed in that direction and found a corner to crouch down in. He thought to himself, *Now I am going insane in my head.*

The soul eater was searching for him. He could sense it. Any demon that was looking for him, he could sense it. He could make out the voices of Asmodeus and Edward, but he knew he couldn't make a sound for fear that the soul eater would find him.

What the hell did I get myself into? Did I really need this? I have to find the bartender, and this shit is keeping me from that mission. I can't fail Mick. That was my promise to her.

Suddenly, he realized his physical surroundings. He wondered if he could make them realize he was still here, just trapped inside his head. *God, that sounds like some weird shit.* Sully tried to reach Edward as he knew they had a brotherly bond, but not a strong one and, well, he didn't trust Asmodeus. Somehow, he could sense Edward and with intense concentration, he forced his arm to rise and reach for Edward's hand. He could grab hold and squeeze, hoping that he could sense him and try to help him.

Sully waited. Then he felt it. The smallest squeeze, but he knew it was Edward. Probably hoping he would know what to do. Then he felt the soul eater. There was no place to run. No place to hide. Sully stood up, even though the shadowy figure motioned for him to stay down.

"No. I am not afraid."

The soul eater approached him. After what seemed to be a quiet standoff, the soul eater moved forward. Sully did not want to show fear, but he was very much afraid.

This was out of his realm. His once normal, demon hunting world has now turned upside down in less than three weeks with coming back home to Scotland, meeting his father for the first time, and learning the true nature of his mother. But he realized that the secret must remain hidden. He didn't know how he knew that, he just did. It was just a matter of time. Sully continued to stand his ground. The soul eater didn't have to come closer. Sully felt his grip. Tighter and tighter. It was like a hammer crushing his brain, not to mention the physical pain he was feeling in his body at the same time. Cupping his hands to his ears, he fell to his knees. The soul eater continued, intensifying the pain. Closing his eyes hard, his body, his mind finally surrendered.

"What do you want from me?" Those were the only words that Sully could manage. A battle he was fighting, inside his mind, inside his body. There was no help to come.

The soul eater simply laughed.

"Fool. You don't realize who you are playing with. I am the vessel of Satan. There is no name for me. I serve him. Your father is a mere tool of his. I am his vessel. Satan, Lucifer, whatever you want to call him. He wants you. But only after I get to play with you for a while. There is a part of you that is locked away, a part that only comes from your mother. Do you know who your mother is?"

Sully remained silent.

"Don't worry, toy, I will get that info for Lucifer. He knew there would be a child, but he didn't know who that child would become. But let's play first. We can stay in here as long as your body doesn't give out."

Again, silence was the only reprieve that Sully could give him. A scream, any sound, would only feed into this monster's ego. He hoped that Edward and Asmodeus could figure out something in time. Feeling his body being squeezed and loosened was taking its toll. His body was aching. His mind was still strong, but he knew there would be a limit. You know the saying, the straw that broke the camel's back? That phrase was all that Sully could focus on.

Then it came. The straw.

The soul eater crushed him. It didn't take long. Apparently, he wasn't strong enough for the demon. Bones cracked, his breathing shallow, the pain filled his mind. Finally, he let out a scream.

"I surrender. Take me to your master. Let's get this over with."

The soul eater looked disappointed. Sully studied his face and couldn't make out why. Then he felt a small touch. It was so light that it wasn't even recognized by the soul eater. That touch grew. His whole body was feeling it. Was it Asmodeus? Edward? He felt different. He felt holy again. That was not Asmodeus. It was not Edward. It was something more beautiful, more peaceful than anything else he'd felt in his entire life.

The soul eater pushed harder at him. But it was not enough. Sully stood stronger, not feeble like moments before. He felt warm inside. Closing his eyes, he thrust his hands out, palms facing the soul eater. Then he spoke in a language he barely knew.

He recognized it, but thought nothing of it, in case the soul eater had a way to read his mind. He continued to try his best to keep parts of him shielded, but it was still a thin layer of protection. Until now. As the words came out, a power came from within him unlike any he had ever experienced, and it sent the demon reeling backward in the oblivion. As the demon reeled back, Sully moved forward. The dark shadowy figure continued to watch. With an intense thrust from his hands, the soul eater disintegrated into ashes. The shadowy figure moved closer to Sully as he lowered his hands.

"Who are you?"

The figure still did not say a word. Instead, the figure's hands lowered the hood and revealed the most beautiful face Sully had ever seen. He still did not recognize the face, but the figure touched Sully's left cheek gently. Then Sully knew. He didn't know how he knew; he just did. Flashes appeared in his mind's eye of a mother cradling her newborn. She was beautiful, and he saw them, coming out from the cloak. Her wings. Translucent and amazing. It was her. And he was the newborn. He just knew.

"Mother."

"Son. Repeat the words I say to you, and you will be free. Tell no one you met me. Your life depends upon it. Be the demon hunter you were born to be, but do not swear allegiance to Asmodeus. The Lord will forgive you, as he has forgiven me for loving Asmodeus. I wasn't supposed to fall in love with him, but I did. The allegiance you swore to him. It will destroy you and him. Find the balance to be the hunter the world needs. The hunter of demons. The hunter of angels. Both need balance. Sometimes there needs to be killing of both kinds to make way. You can't stay in Scotland. You need to go back to her, back to the beginning. Finish what you started. Go soon. Go now. It is not safe for you or Edward. Keep Edward close to you, you will need them both to finish your quest. But the journey has just begun now that you have mixed with the soul eater. Now say the words. All of them. It is important that you say all of them. I love the man you have become. Go to the girl. She is the key you seek."

Sully did not understand but repeated what he heard. He was back in the room where this all began. He was back with his father and Edward. But not his mother.

"I saw her," was all he could say before vomiting in front of Asmodeus' feet. Edward reeled back but placed a hand on Sully's lower back. Wiping his mouth, Sully eventually was feeling better. He took a firm look at Asmodeus and said through clenched teeth, "We need to speak now."

Asmodeus nodded and Sully grabbed his arm, pulling him closer so that no one else could hear their conversation. Then he spoke in the language of demons. The words just came to him as if he'd been speaking their language all his life.

"I met her. We can't stay here, father. She told me that. Edward and I have to go back to Los Angeles. There is someone I left behind. Will you aid me, father, in the future? The soul eater is gone, for now, but I sense he will be back."

His father placed a hand on his shoulder and said the words that made Sully quiver. "Son. Call on me and I will come. Keep her presence secret. Tell no one."

A book magically appeared in Asmodeus' hand, and he gave it to Sully. The book appeared to be ancient looking. Besides the book, he handed him another blade, larger than the one he currently owned. This one was different. It had strange symbols on the handle, but Sully recognized them, though he wasn't sure how.

"Take these. You will need these. I sense you are about to discover your true destiny. I have always watched out for you. Let me look into your soul. Please. Allow your father that at least."

Sully nodded and opened himself to Asmodeus. He felt his presence with a slight amount of discomfort because, in all his years, he never once let a demon inside his soul. Yet this was different. This was his father. A demon. And he was a demon's son. And an angel's son. Once he felt Asmodeus pull out of his soul, the discomfort vanished.

Asmodeus sat down on the cold, hard floor. For a demon that stood six feet tall, strong with broad shoulders and dark wings, he sat there with tears streaming down his cheeks. Sully stared at him with wonder and then looked at Edward. He shrugged, not knowing what to say or do but remembering that he was more than just a demon hunter—he was also a monk in a previous lifetime.

"Asmodeus, I mean, Father, what did you see? Is my soul as black as your wings because of the soul eater? Tell me! I have a right to know. If I die today, I must choose the Lord above you, above my mother."

Asmodeus choked back a tear. "Son, your mother left you something of hers inside you. I don't know how or what it is, but it is there. Locked away and I'm sure it will open to you when you need it most. The soul eater lives inside your soul. Small but strong. It is going to feed on you. You won't notice it at first, but over time, it will drain you. Your power, your immortality, your life. I failed you. But I sense that an organization created to destroy both Heaven and Hell contacted you. I see it in your eyes. You must stay away from them. Edward filled me in that Margaret contacted you."

Sully couldn't believe what he was hearing. Just last month, he was living a normal life, well, not entirely normal, but the life he was used to living for centuries and now his days kept getting better and better. He was sarcastic about this.

"Shit." That's all he could say while he continued to look down at the ground.

"Father, Edward and I have to leave Scotland then. I... I don't know what to say. I grew up not understanding myself or my true nature, and I still don't. There is something about her that I must protect. And I can't protect you either if I stay here, especially with Margaret being a lie. What is this damn organization? They found me."

Sully couldn't take much more before he finally broke down. He felt defeated, though not sure from what. Sully felt both Asmodeus' and Edward's hands on him and a surge of electricity pulsed through his body. At least it felt like electricity. The amount of energy that coursed through his veins made him feel different. It raised him into the air and as he opened his eyes, he looked down at the lifeless body of the abbot. The poor man had not survived his fate, yet he still lived. He always hated this part. His immortality. When he reached the ground once more, he was not the same. He was different, but he didn't know how.

He hastened to his open bag and took out another vial of Holy Water. This was his most sacred and important vial in all his collection. He'd kept it with him for as long as he could remember, even when he was a brother monk. Sully opened it and allowed one precious drop to touch his finger. He wanted to be sure he was still himself. It didn't burn him. In fact, the drop vanished into his skin and awakened something inside him. Something that was asleep for a long time.

"What did you do to me?"

Asmodeus smiled. "I made sure that you inherited all your parental genes, and not just that of your mother's. Let's just say I kept the parts you inherited dormant. This was to keep you safe. Your mother wanted you protected until you were old enough to face the truth of your destiny. You have a purpose. You must find her. She is the key. Both your mother and I, which is why we gave you up closely guarded that secret. Do not let Margaret get her hands on the girl."

"Wait… what? My destiny? What girl? I didn't ask for any of this. To be born the son of an angel and demon. *Who* the fuck am I or *what* am I? What happened to the most absolute law between Heaven and Hell? That demons and angels will not produce offspring. It could not be."

Asmodeus sighed. "It was, my son. Until I met your mother. You don't know your demon history as well as you should. But there is no time for that. The organization that brought you here located you. They are coming for you, and this time they will not be kind. We need to get you out of here, and quickly. Edward, you know what to do."

Asmodeus somehow made an opening appear in the wall that wasn't there before. Rather than waiting around to run into Margaret, Sully reached for his bag and made haste through the door. Before taking his last step through the door, he gave the dead abbot one last look and silently prayed for his soul. Edward followed him and last, Asmodeus. The three were running away from the monastery and found a nearby taxi waiting for them. Sully looked at the driver and saw the same demon mark he had, representing Asmodeus.

Sully, wasting no time and wanting to get out of Scotland, quickly told the driver to take them to the airport. While en route to the airport, he talked to Edward and Asmodeus about how they were going to leave the country. He noticed that Asmodeus just smiled and laughed. Something that made him very uncomfortable. The three rode in silence the rest of the way, but Sully was lost in thought. It had distracted him from his mission to find the bartender, and his thoughts turned to Mick.

Somehow, his mother's warning took hold. He needed her. Why? She was beautiful, even though she was distressed. Something attracted him to her despite the vows made a very long time ago. It was tormenting him, but he kept this little fact secret.

The taxi drove fast heading to the airport, but the car ran over something and flipped over repeatedly. Sully was thrown from the car just moments before he glimpsed flames from an explosion. His father. His brother. The driver. Were they alive? Before he could move, he blacked out.

CHAPTER 11

"Find him. Search everywhere. If you find anyone else, bring them too. My father and uncle will be pleased that we have the demon hunter."

Sully couldn't open his eyes, but he knew that voice. He remained still but wondered about the driver, Asmodeus, and even Edward. Then he knew he was the only one because someone yelled that there was no one else in the area. He felt a small tear trickle down his cheek as he thought of the driver. Another one of his father's loyal servants. A voice rang in his head.

"Son, we are safe, and you still breathe. Don't let the bitch take you. If you do, you will not serve your destiny if you end up in that organization. Feel the power I gave you. Let it guide you."

Sully kept his eyes closed and tried to drown out the sounds from all around him. Luckily, they were not near him yet, but it was only a matter of time. What was it that his father said? As much as he thought of Asmodeus, he couldn't quite get used to the idea of calling him father. He had a father that raised him, loved him.

Sully slowed his breathing to the brink of falling into a meditative state. He reached inside himself. His mind made him think he was floating inside his body, searching for something. He saw the soul eater, lying dormant for now. Then he felt a power unlike any other he'd felt before. Sully let that power consume his being. He felt stronger, more powerful, and somehow full of understanding of angels and demons. This must have been what Asmodeus gave him.

A touch on his cheek disturbed his meditative state and brought him back to reality. He kept his eyes closed but could sense those near him. He waited.

"Bring the mask to cover his head. Then lift him and put him in the Range Rover. As long as he stays unconscious, we should be able to make it to the compound. We can start programming him then. And tie his hands! He is the demon hunter and the son of a demon."

He felt his head being lifted but gave no sign of being alert. He continued to let the power fill him with a force that he didn't quite understand. But if he could hear his father, he was stronger now than he was when he woke up earlier today. Sully knew he couldn't let them take him back to the compound, but never in his life had he ever been in this predicament. Usually, he was the victor in all things. He waited, but he would not ignore his father's pleas to not get caught.

Hands hoisted him up, placed the mask over his head and, once they had done that, he opened his eyes. Pitch black. Darkness. They carried him to the vehicle and once they were about to hoist him into the seat, he squinted his eyes and before he realized it—the mask disintegrated. He could look directly into the eyes of the man he recognized from the hotel. The man was one of Margaret's guards. Before the guard could utter a sound, he stared straight into his eyes and whispered one word in the demonic language. *Die.* The man dropped.

Sully couldn't believe what had just happened. It gave him chills. But there was no time to spare. The other man was reaching for his weapon. He whispered another word to the man. *Burn.* The man was set in flames. So, now, he was more than a demon hunter. He was a killer. Would it matter at this point? This was his life and it was now spinning seriously out of control. He went from demon hunter to son of both an angel and a demon to a killer. Definitely not honoring his vow to God. But now was not the time to think about it. Sully had to get out of this predicament if he truly believed the words of Asmodeus.

He didn't hear anyone else come near the vehicle, so he slowly climbed out and leaned against the car, watching to see where the others were. Then he saw her.

Margaret. The bitch. He took another look inside the car for a weapon and saw nothing of use. Then he remembered his blade. Taking it out from his back pocket, he gripped the handle tightly and prepared to use it on anyone that would get in his way.

Then he saw Malcolm. He remembered him. He'd promised Malcolm to keep his real name a secret. Sully tried to get his attention and when he finally did, Malcolm was making his way over to him.

"Sully. You're awake. Where are the other guards?"

"Dead, burned. I met Asmodeus. I can't let Margaret take me back. What in the world is she doing here?"

Malcolm pushed Sully further back into the side of the car and Sully was trying to push him off, to no avail. But he relaxed his body, remembering that Malcolm served his father. Malcolm placed his hand over Sully's mouth, urging him to be quiet. Sully strained his ears, but he could hear Margaret approaching. It was a matter of minutes.

Margaret must have been quicker than he expected because before he or Malcolm realized it, she was standing right by them, holding a pistol straight to his chest.

"Oh, shit."

He could hear Margaret laughing and calling him an imbecile demon hunter. Sully couldn't take much more of this and raised his blade to meet the end of her pistol. Little did she know his blade was also made from diamonds and not just steel. It was his own personal combination, along with a few added kicks from spells he picked up over the years. He nudged the tip into the pistol some, just to give her a feeling that he wasn't kidding around. The blade sprang to life and just as he knew it would, it sent a little "greeting" through her pistol and into her hands, forcing her to drop the pistol.

"You think your blade is going to save you, Sully? That was just a little shock I wasn't prepared for. Better you find out about us now rather than going through the introductions in the compound. After all, I wouldn't want them to mess up that good-looking face of yours."

"Margaret, I know who I am. I don't need you or your kind to tell me. Let me show you."

With that said, Sully lowered his blade and put it down on the ground. Closing his eyes, he took a deep breath and another. On the third breath, he opened his eyes and said, "Asmodeus."

His father appeared behind Margaret and placed his hand on her back. Margaret didn't move. Sully looked at his father and shouted, "What the fuck are you doing?"

Asmodeus smiled. "I only froze her. She can still hear us, see us, but she just can't move, and she can't call for backup."

He caught his father nodding to Malcolm. Malcolm did not show reverence for his master because to do so would be to blow his cover. Sully had only moments to think about what to do next and to make sure that Asmodeus did not get the upper hand in this. His heart was beating fast, anxiety going through the roof. He had an idea, but one he knew would be risky. Telepathically, he sent a message to his father and Malcolm, not even sure he knew he could do this, but he gave it his best shot. His only shot. He told them to play along and he would be safe, to trust him. Malcolm nodded, eventually followed by Asmodeus.

Sully bent down and picked up his blade, never taking his eyes off Margaret.

"Alright, Margaret. My father is behind you. He will release you from his control. In exchange for your life, my father is going to send you somewhere, anywhere, far away from here. And it won't be back at your compound. But understand this, I am NOT the same person you met in Los Angeles. I know exactly who I am now. And what my true power is. I am my father's heir and that is something you cannot control. Father, send her far away. I don't care where, but I will take all her coms and firearms first." He said this, while seething in his teeth, to show how ruthless he could be. Then, he stripped her of all weapons, com devices, and patted her down once more to be sure.

Nodding to Asmodeus, he gave the signal to make her disappear. Asmodeus released his control on Margaret. She made a movement towards Sully, but before he could react, his father made her disappear. Sully breathed a sigh of relief as he collapsed to the ground. Malcolm tried to catch him, but he was a little slow in responding. His head was pounding and there was a loud ringing in his ears. Sully cupped his hands around his ears as his nose bled. He saw his father kneel to him, placing his arm on his shoulders as if to comfort him. The ringing wouldn't stop. Finally, he blacked out.

***

Margaret found herself lost in a forest, unharmed, and she was certainly not happy about this. She thought that this was the first time in her life that she felt confused, betrayed, and isolated from all that she was trained to believe in. Sully had actually called upon the demon prince Asmodeus. Things were taking a more complicated turn than she would've liked. After a few minutes of walking around on her own, she tried to call the organization. They didn't take her phone which was hidden in a pocket, but the call didn't go through either. As she looked down at her phone, she saw there was no signal. She wandered for hours, aimlessly searching for someone to help her.

A demon appeared, startling her. She remained cool, calm, and collected. "What do you want?"

"A chance to talk with you. Do you know who I am?"

Margaret shook her head, displeased with this intrusion. "I'm afraid I don't but you're connected to Sully somehow, aren't you?"

The demon laughed. "I want the hunter. You want the hunter. I'm Balam. I'm sure you have heard of me. I will send you wherever you want to go, on one condition. You are now in my service and together we will crush the hunter."

Margaret was not pleased to be in any alliance with a demon. Using her training, she caught him unaware and had him in a chokehold before he could do anything else. She didn't kill him, just made him unconscious. She knew she couldn't kill Balam, but her training taught her to subdue demons. It just happened to be a brutal fight before he went down. This was her mission. And her target was Sully. An uncooperative but desirable demon hunter.

CHAPTER 12

When Sully came to several hours later, he was surprised to find himself back in the monastery, under the careful watch of the monks. There was no sign of Asmodeus or Malcolm, but he was partially naked under the sheets and his head was throbbing. Edward was sitting in a chair, watching over him. A monk was wiping his forehead with a cool cloth. A bowl of broth was on the nightstand and once the monk saw he was awake, he reached for the bowl and spoon.

He tried to prop himself up on the pillow to make it easier for the monk to feed him. Edward must have seen the movement and hurried over to his side. Sully gave him a little smile. He felt very weak but managed a few spoons of the broth before letting the monk know that he'd had enough for now. But he made sure to let the monk know he was thankful with a kind smile. The monk left the room, after writing on the tablet that he would let the others know he was awake and would return. Sully smiled.

Once alone, he asked Edward what happened.

"Brother, father brought you here because your injuries were not something he could fix. He and Malcolm left to return below, but your injuries were not from his side. He told you to find the girl. She holds the answers. I'm just glad you are not dead. When can we go back?"

"I don't know. I feel weak. What happened to me?"

"I thought you could tell me so I can tell father. He thinks it has something to do with Margaret. I knew I didn't like her."

His head was pounding, but the few spoons of broth helped a little. He sat even more upright, but it started again. The ringing in his ears. When the ringing stopped, he relaxed a little. He couldn't make sense of this. What the fuck was going on with him? His thoughts were interrupted when the brother returned with two more monks. Through the writing tablets, they wanted to know about the abbot. Was he saved or not?

Apparently, these monks knew more about the abbot's condition than they let on. One of them handed a tablet to him so that he could tell them what had happened. On it were the words "Do not make a sound. The brother that fed you the broth is a traitor. You must get your strength and run."

Sully thought to himself, *Out of the fire and into the frying pan.* It couldn't get any worse…or could it? He wiped off the message, considering how to respond. Then he wrote. Fast and furiously. *The abbot is dead. Something evil is here in the monastery.* He handed it back to the monk, who gave him the tablet. Sully noticed he read it and then showed it to the others.

The monks looked horrified except for the one identified as the traitor. There was something about him. Finally, Sully decided to just break the rule of the monastery, since he already had broken so many of their rules. He spoke.

"I am the demon hunter from 1329, from this very monastery. You can't kill me. You can't hurt me. But I can help you. Let me back into the room where the exorcisms took place. Evil is here."

Before showing him to the room, the monks gave him the privacy to dress. It was the same room, regardless of the past or present. The abbot's body still lay on the floor, untouched. Sully motioned for the monks to take and prepare the body for a proper burial. They did, and they left the room as quickly as they entered it, leaving him and Edward all alone.

"Edward, I am going to need you. I bought us time, but one of those three is a traitor. That's what the one brother was telling me on the tablet. Teach me what father did to escape. It's our only way."

Edward reviewed and showed Sully how to make a doorway in the wall, just like before. It made Sully a little weak, probably from all the crazy shit that had just happened to him recently, but he shook it off and both he and Edward left the monastery. This time, instead of traveling down the path as they had done earlier, Sully went in the opposite direction. His only mission was to get out of Scotland and back to Mick. Somehow, he knew the answers would be there.

Sully kept urging Edward on, sometimes forgetting that his demon brother was in a child-size body. The one thing that he didn't have on him at the moment was his bag of tools. Making his way around the monastery, he found where the car accident happened. Luckily, for him, it didn't cause any unwanted attention because of the secluded nature of the monastery.

He searched the road looking for his bag and he found it. Not too far from where he'd been thrown. But then he caught the smell. Demons. And not friendly ones. Grabbing his bag, he threw it over his shoulder and hoisted Edward onto his shoulders and made quick strides to find his way out of the area as soon as possible. He didn't even concern himself with Margaret, her whereabouts, or anything with the organization. As they made their way closer to the town, Sully found the town hall, and just like the driver said, it was near the bakery. His stomach growled. Sully figured that he and Edward should stop and devour something.

They finished and made their way to the town hall. The receptionist was friendly and very helpful in assisting them with the records from the past. He was given quite a few old-looking books to go through. She explained that not all the books made it to microfilm yet because of the time and experience it required, which was scarce since the town was so small. Sully thanked her and promised he would be extra careful with the books. He would return them in the same condition that she gave them to him when he was done. Edward and Sully took a table in the back and combed through the books.

He found the records for the monastery, including his name on a list. He ran his finger over his name and got sentimental about this, probably being the only record with his name from all those centuries ago. Then he noticed Edward looking at him with a hint of sadness on his face. Edward spoke.

"I didn't realize that your life is so hard, Sully. Brother. I took it for granted, but seeing you just now made me think that this is difficult. Now with father being Asmodeus and this organization and all. I'm sorry I make things hard for you."

Sully appreciated the sentiment and told him it was ok. They had work to do together, and Sully even apologized to Edward for being cruel to him over the centuries. It was the start of brotherly love.

Hours went by and as he looked through book after book, he found some pages that interested him. It was documented about the monastery being involved with exorcisms and the organization. But the year was not 1329. It was around the 1500s. According to this, Mary de Guise was believed to have been instrumental in the organization's development of learning more about "such things that exist but are not openly discussed" was how it was carefully worded.

Mary de Guise? This was certainly interesting. He kept reading. The English Monarchy was involved? United States? Many countries, many humans. He asked Edward to get some paper and a pen, as they had notes to take immediately before leaving. Edward left and returned with a lot of paper and two pens.

Sully frantically took notes, lots of notes. He couldn't believe the amount of historical key figures that were part of the organization's grip around the world. Margaret wasn't kidding when she tried to tell him about how long they'd existed. Humans knew about demons that walked the earth? Incredible! Not to mention she'd lied to him.

Then he saw it.

He decided not to react when he saw Edward's name. His real name. The one name he would not tell Sully. He read a little more about his brother. Instead of writing it down, in case Edward saw, he memorized all he learned. Until he could ask later. Too many questions flew through his mind, but the one stood out: How does he fit in with the organization? What is his connection to the secret Asmodeus was trying to tell him about? And his conscience weighed on. Sully was a demon hunter. It was all he knew. Should he continue to kill his own kind? And his mother. The biggest secret of all.

As he walked along the wall, Sully tried to stay away from the windows. Then he saw six men coming toward the town hall. "We're about to have company soon," he said quietly to Edward. He moved closer to the front of the room to get a better look. He couldn't tell if they were from the organization or something else.

Then Sully smelled them. Demons. *Shit.* Here we go again.

CHAPTER 13

Sully pulled Edward closer, whispering, "Brother, when we get out of here, you and I are going to have a long overdue talk."

Giving Edward a few vials, he motioned for him to hide and be prepared. Sully then took the receptionist and told her to hide. It was going to get very nasty. She did as she was told. Then, finding a marker on her desk, he drew a symbol on the floor. Throwing another one of his vials on it, he called upon a demon he had a longstanding bargain with. While waiting for that demon to appear, he closed his eyes and searched his mind. He was trying to feel for that damn soul eater.

Then he found it.

"Are you looking for me, demon hunter?"

Sully gulped. He didn't want to wake it because he couldn't deal with the physical pain right now that it would cause. He whispered what he wanted, in his mind, to the soul eater and before he could open his eyes, his body was taken over by it. Silently, he remained inside, but he could see what was happening all around him and he felt strength and power unlike anything he'd known before. He knew the soul eater was in control, though they shared the same body. This would be interesting.

He watched as the demons approached. Sully was not used to being in the passenger seat, but he needed help from an unlikely ally. Maybe call this an unholy alliance. As he thought about it, the soul eater started laughing.

"I knew you would see things my way, demon hunter. Son of Asmodeus."

Sully allowed the soul eater control of his body. He watched as he approached the demons.

"What do you want?"

The demons looked at Sully. Sully fought the urge to take back control of his body. He waited. He watched.

The soul eater spoke, using Sully's voice. "I say again, what do you want, demons of Hell?"

"We came for you."

The soul eater laughed and then stood in the open doorway, unarmed. Silently, Sully was praying about having made the right decision to trust the soul eater. He fought against relinquishing control but found that he was losing. The soul eater was much too tough and somehow could multitask against him and an onset of demons coming his way. Sully cowered in the corner of his mind. Waiting.

The soul eater cursed at the demons. One of them was set on fire and the flames prevented him from. He didn't disintegrate into ashes, but he remained on fire in front of the others. Thrusting his hand outward, he said another curse. One that Sully knew all too well. Another demon froze in his spot.

The other demons still moved forward. Finally, the soul eater whispered to Sully. "Join me." Sully did not understand but allowed his mind to merge with the soul eater. He was in full control of his body once more. But something inside snapped. An intense heat filled his body from the inside and as he shouted out a curse, the remaining demons fell to their knees. Sully walked over to them. Looked at them closely.

"You. You are the ones I saw that took the bartender. Where is he?"

The demons laughed and they tried to stand to no avail. They were not able to stand. From the corner of his eye, Sully noticed that Edward had taken up in the corner and looked scared. He demanded that he come out. It was time to end this.

"Edward, there's always a price to pay for this. Come out here now."

He saw Edward come out, and he held onto the vial that he'd given him previously. He whispered to the soul eater, "The bargain is simple. I will exist with you if you agree to join forces with me. You and I will become one. But you will not betray me and turn me over like you originally planned to do. In return, you can slowly feed on my soul to survive, but you will not kill me. I am already a tormented soul. You and I will make our own path. Let's call this an unholy alliance. What say you?"

The soul eater spoke through Sully's lips.

"The deal is agreed. What about Edward? Can I have the little demon too?"

Sully saw Edward was afraid. "No. He is not to be touched or I will use the very power from both sides to kill you and send you back to Hell. Now, deal with them. I need them to find the bartender."

Together, they merged into one. Sully only hoped that he'd made the right choice, but time was not on his side. He motioned to Edward to give him the vial. Holding the vials carefully in his hands, he was thinking about what to do. He allowed himself to trust the soul eater, and he opened the vials, one by one. He then threw the vials at the demons. They did not die. They remained still, not moving, not speaking. Sully saw they could look around and noticed that their eyes changed.

"Obey." That was the only word out of Sully's mouth.

The demons knelt and looked straight at Sully. All that came out of their mouths was, "The soul eater." Then they vanished. Something must've called them back to Hell.

"Shit."

But somehow, this did not faze him as much as he thought. Maybe the soul eater had a plan? Sully needed to learn to merge with the soul eater in everything. He'd made the deal after all, and this was no time to play rank. Sully found the receptionist and calmed her down.

"What are you?"

Sully responded, "I'm Sully. Demon hunter and something more now, I suppose. Who knows? There is an organization here. Something centuries old that had key figures linked per the books I found. How much does this town know?"

She straightened her glasses and tried to adjust her clothing in its previous disarrayed state. She gave him a blank stare, as if she did not understand him. Sully had no time for this. He had to get back to Los Angeles after everything that happened here.

"Lady don't mess with me. I am not in the mood. You seem to know more than you are letting on. So, I will fill you in. See this ring on my finger? I am the son of Asmodeus, and you don't want to know who my mother is. Being his son is proof enough. I am a demon hunter, and well, I am now merged with a demon called the soul eater. My father will not be pleased. So, I am going to ask you once more. What does this town know?"

She took a piece of paper, wrote something on it, folded it and handed it to him.

He read it. *There are eyes everywhere. The organization is everywhere.* Then she handed him another note that she quickly wrote by saying, "This is the title of the book you are looking for, sir. It gives you an appreciation for our town's architecture. The book would be on the other side of the room. If you will excuse me, I must clean up the office."

Sully took the paper and read the note. *Go to the other side of the room. Pull the lever that is behind the statue. Secret room no one knows exists, Son of Asmodeus.*

Sully stared at her in disbelief. The woman knew who he was. He wondered if everyone he would come across would know his true identity.. Then he looked down at his hand and saw the ring. Of course. Anyone who knows Asmodeus would recognize his ring. The ring was a sign of who he was. The son of Asmodeus. His mind moved to thoughts of Mick. Her dark hair, her piercing eyes, and there was something about her beauty that captivated him. He never allowed himself to fall for a woman before because of his vow to God, yet Mick was different. Even the thought of her lips gave him a sense of desire. And the vow. Forgetting where he was, he allowed himself a small smile until he caught Edward staring at him.

"Edward, I have to look for this book over there. You liked the buildings a lot, it will tell us who designed them. Come."

He could tell Edward was confused, but he made sure Edward followed. He had his bag in hand. Sully whispered to the soul eater that he must be in control now. But if he needed him, he would ask. They were going to have to find out how to make this new partnership work.

They walked across the room, found the lever, and Sully opened a secret door. They both went inside and the door closed. Flipping the light switch, he could see the room more clearly. Old parchments, books, weapons and more filled the room. Edward's face lit up. He ran to some parchments and combed through them. Sully told him to be careful, so he put them back.

Edward grabbed for Sully's hand, and it gave him a sort of comforting feeling. Family. Brothers. Sully went to the table and looked through the parchment. He could read them. These were ancient prophecies and because he still had the book that his father gave him, he laid it on the table. Opening it, he flipped through the pages. Then he noticed some pages were missing. He wondered. He started going through the parchments.

Time passed and he must've lost track because, before he knew it, the receptionist was standing behind him.

"Did you find what you were looking for, Son of Asmodeus? It is safe to talk in here."

Sully showed her the book and the disarray of parchments.

He asked her plainly, "How do these fit in with the book? You already know who I am, so call me Sully."

"Well, Sully, there are prophecies belonging to Heaven and Hell. Each side with its own prophecy. There is to be the final last war between Heaven and Hell, although no one knows when that will be. Both sides have been preparing for it, but the time is not near, otherwise, it would've happened by now. Let me see your book."

She took the book and started thumbing through it. Sully thought she must be familiar with it by the way she handled it. Grabbing a parchment from the table that had ripped edges, she inserted it into one of its pages and the page was fully restored. Handing it back to him, she told him to read the page.

Sully sat down, and Edward hovered near him. He read it.

A child, an heir to both Heaven and Hell, will rise above all. A key, forged in an ancient battle by the demons, will unlock both passages to Heaven and Hell. Together, the heir will yield the key to prevent the annihilation of both demons and angels by a force so dark......

The rest of the passage was faded, and he couldn't make it out. The child of Heaven and Hell. Hmm.

"The rest is faded. I can't finish the prophecy."

"It's not faded. It's not meant to be read yet. The rest of the passage will make itself known when it is the right time. Your father's books are rather special. I assume he gave this one to you, otherwise the page would not have been restored."

Sully nodded.

The woman said, "This book, once touched by the heir of Asmodeus, cannot leave his side. You must always carry this book with you. It will reveal information to you as you need it to. Simply open the book. It will do the rest. It was made for you. Or didn't you know that?"

Sully shook his head no. Too much, he obviously didn't know, but why? Then she said that it was time to close the town hall, but that there was an exit to the outside of this room when they were ready to leave. She left.

Sully looked at Edward, more confused than ever.

"Edward, I hate this shit. First, I was a hunter of demons. That's all I was. Then, I am heir to Asmodeus. And my mother…"

Sully stopped short of revealing that to Edward, but then he said, "It's pointless to keep this from you. I am going to need you by my side. I was always a hunter. *The* hunter of demons. Now, I am the heir to Asmodeus. Of what, who knows? And you might as well know. My mother is an archangel. My birth should never have happened. I don't know what that side of me is like. My world is just not the way it used to be."

Edward came over and put his hand on Sully's shoulder. He could feel the sensitivity in that touch from Edward.

"Brother, yeah, it's crazy now, but think of the good you can do for this world. I'm not an evil demon, I mean, sure, you tried many times to kill me, but I always came back. My purpose was to always be at your side when you were ready. I think you are ready now. What if we took some of these parchments and went back to the states?"

Sully looked through the parchments once more and knew he had to decide. They had to leave Scotland, no matter what.

"Let's look through these to see what's what and grab the ones we think will be useful. Then we are out of here. We must find a way back to Los Angeles."

CHAPTER 14

One week later, Sully was walking into the bar. He was nervous about seeing Mick, especially with no signs of her friend. But he had to reach out to her.

Standing at the doorway, he saw her slinging drinks with such finesse for a group of drunks. She looked up and saw him. There was a sparkle in her eye. A sense of hope. Better he let her know before walking to the bar in hopes she would remain calm. He shook his head, trying to signal to her that her friend was not found.

He found an empty stool at the counter and before he sat down, his shot glass was waiting for him. Ah, gin. It had never tasted so good before. Before he could put the glass down, Mick was already waiting to give him a refill.

"You didn't find him. Is he dead?"

Sully downed another shot. "Can you leave the bar now, or are you working all by yourself? We need to talk."

Mick must've taken the hint and told someone else that she was ending her shift now. She had a family emergency. She grabbed her coat and was already waiting for Sully. He paid the bill and met her at the door. He told her they were going to her friend's apartment, where this all started. Silence on the entire way there. Déjà vu.

"Sully, what is going on? You're scaring me. Is he dead? He is, isn't he?" she cried. Then he saw it. Between her index finger and thumb. It was a strange marking. Could it be a birthmark? Sully didn't recall how he knew what it was, he just knew.

He grabbed her hand, startling her, but she trusted him as he pulled it closer. He needed a better look, squinting his eye. Mick pulled her hand back, demanding to know what he was looking at.

"I've had that all my life. It's some kind of birthmark. Stop being a creeper."

***

Mick looked down at her birthmark, thinking it was the one thing about herself that always made her self-conscious about her looks. She didn't care that she was more gothic looking than some women, always dressed in black, and even kept a small knife hidden in the seams of her skirt. She rubbed her birthmark out of habit as if trying to erase it.

She never thought about her childhood, because it always made her disgusted at the system, and because of that, men made her feel awkward at times. Sully scared her and that brought back memories of one of the foster homes, but she tried to hide it. Changing the subject, she began to question Sully. It was her turn to ask the questions.

"Is he dead? Is that what you're not telling me, why we had to come here? I knew it. I just knew something bad happened to him."

She stood up in frustration and tried to get Sully to answer but he didn't. Instead, he rose and took her hands in his, and gently sat her down. It was an act of sensitivity that sparked something in her that she couldn't quite put into words.

***

Sully told her to sit down and listen as he explained everything. Something inside him told him that he could trust her. He wondered if it was knowing his mother told him to return to Mick. Regardless, Sully always relied on his gut and instinct to guide him.

"Mick, there are things in this world that most people ignore or don't believe in. Demons and angels are some of those things. I am a demon hunter. I hunt demons. In fact, my father is the demon Asmodeus. It's a long story that I will tell you." He told his story.

By the time he was done talking about demon hunting and the parchments, he saw it was too much for her. Mick had her hands over her face, tears streaming down.

Sully got his pack and removed the book. He opened it and tried to show her. Taking her hands away from her face, he brushed away the tears from her cheeks. And as gently as he could, he said, "Look at this book. This is my world."

He turned page after page, but she looked at him puzzled.

"The pages are blank. I thought you were cool, but you're a freak. God damn you. I hate you."

***

Mick felt betrayed by trusting him and then making her listen to these fairytales. She had enough but then she noticed it. His features softened as if he truly did not mean to scare her.

"If you are a demon hunter, and there are demons in this world, then where are the angels? Aren't angels supposed to be here to protect us from them?"

Mick couldn't hold back the tears but again, she looked into his eyes and the tenderness was there. Maybe she could give him a chance and hear him out, despite the past when she was constantly hurt by men. She didn't want to think of the pain that caused her so she decided to listen to him more. She wanted to know more. There was something about him that made her feel connected although she didn't know what.

***

Sully stood back and told her, "God already did. But there is something about you. What is it? You can't be a demon or I would have smelled that. You don't smell like my mother, but similar. What are you exactly?"

Sully took her hand in his, and instinct told him to put their hands on the book, together. The book shook before revealing its pages to Mick. Sully pulled it closer to him to read the pages. He realized Mick may not be able to read the words or symbols. Recalling what he'd learned in the town hall about unlocking the passages of Heaven and Hell it didn't take long for Sully to put two and two together about Mick. Maybe he also knew from the way his mother urged him to "go back to the girl". Was she the key? He read the pages to Mick.

"Tell me about your parents, Mick. I am not trying to scare you or hurt you. But there is something about you. Something more than just your beauty."

"I never had parents. The foster care system was where I grew up. I was unwanted by everyone till I aged out. Not even foster parents kept me for more than a few months at a time. You're really scaring me, you know. But there's something different about you now than when I first met you." Tears flowed down her cheeks as she spoke to him. Her voice was soft and quivering.

Feeling a little embarrassed about that last part, he tried to focus but couldn't. She was beautiful. Each time he looked at her, he felt drunk on her beauty. Mick looked at him and her hand reached for his face. He let her guide his mouth to hers. She made the first move. He couldn't. He tried to stop her, remembering his vow to God, but something else took over. Instinct.

Her skin was soft. Her lips were also soft against his, partly opening as her tongue flicked against his. After all these centuries, it took Mick to get him to release his guard. To release him from his centuries-old promise. He kept his eyes closed and tried to copy what Mick was doing, but she pulled away.

"Is this like your first kiss or something?"

Sully laughed. "I guess it is. A long time ago, I made a promise, and I was a monk. I serve God. And now, I hunt demons. But you. There is something about you. You got me to betray my promise to God and when we touched, the book came to life. You're not human. Maybe a half-breed?"

Mick looked at him, probably thinking that he lost his damn mind. Who knows? She didn't respond verbally to him. Her response was more passionate, full of lust. She leaned her body into his, pressing hers against his. He could feel her thigh against his manhood. It came to life as she kissed him more intensely this time. She threw him down and looked directly into his eyes.

"I can live in your mind and heart, coming alive when you need me most," she said as she lingered down his body and then knelt on her knees.

Sully didn't continue as her words struck deep. Then he remembered. *Damn*. His father was Asmodeus, the demon of lust. With all his body has been through in the last month, could he be feeding her somehow with lust? Then she spoke again. "Hunter. Come to me. Surrender yourself to me. Yield your sword in my name."

Sully looked closely at Mick. Her eyes were no longer her own. Her body was no longer her own. Mick was possessed. She reached for him again. He let her fold her body into his. Then, reaching for his knife, he made a small nick on her thumb. Not deep, but enough to cause her to scream. Sully used this time to call upon his brother.

Edward appeared. Mick cowered away in what seemed to Sully like a ploy. He knew demon possession when he saw it, but this was something different. Something, unlike anything he had encountered before. Could Mick be a half-breed too? Or something more? He moved closer to comfort her, and then he noticed it once more. That birthmark. It was strangely familiar, but he couldn't recall from where he had seen it.

"Who is that?"

"Edward, this is Mick. What I can't figure out is if she's a demon, possessed, or something else. It could be anything. But her words. Her words are calling to me somehow. Maybe I need to get out of here, but we never finished talking about the bartender. Things just got messy."

Edward walked towards her. Edward reached his hand out to Mick and Sully saw her take it before pulling back. Sully fumbled through his bag and took out one of his holy relics used to exorcise demons. Not all those possessed deserved to be killed to be rid of a demon. He tried to save the humans. He looked at the pink solution in the vial. It had a certain glow to it that made it mesmerizing.

"Mick, drink this. It won't hurt you, but it might save you." He handed her the vial, thinking she was in control, and he let it go in her hand. Only to find that she flung it across the room, breaking it.

"Oh hunter, poor hunter. You want this body back, don't you? Then solve this little riddle. From the skies comes the light. From below the earth comes the fire. I am the in-between, the doorway without a key. Name me and stand by my side."

Sully laughed. He was tempted because deep down he knew this was Mick and he had a certain fondness for her. The demon wanted to play with him and Mick while Edward watched. Then he saw something in Edward change. Edward became Asmodeus, causing Sully to shield his body to protect Mick.

"Come forth, Abaddon. Leave this girl alone. She is nothing to you. She is not the key you seek. Leave her body now or suffer my wrath."

The demon laughed hysterically and left Mick's body. Sully couldn't believe what he was seeing. His father. Here in Los Angeles. His head was spinning with all this craziness. But he gathered his strength, leaving Mick's side and standing up to face his father.

"I summoned Edward. Not you, father."

"Son, I came because of Edward. He sought my help, and I will always come to your aid. This girl. This child. Who is she?"

"This is Mick. The bartender's friend asked for my help. And I will save her friend, even if I have to spend time in Hell to find him."

Asmodeus bent down and placed a finger under her chin. He lifted it up to look into her eyes. Sully came closer for a look. The demon was gone. Abaddon. The worst demon in all of Hell. Sully was feeling the toll from these games that were being played with him. Rage filled his soul. Asmodeus must've felt something because he placed his hand on Sully's shoulder and simply said the word, "Volo."

Sully had no choice but to obey Asmodeus. He heard the word and his guard went down against his father. But then something snapped. Inside, his body felt warm with a strong power of grace. His shoulders were aching. He closed his eyes and screamed. Opening them, he saw that the room was black. He saw his father, but nothing else. No Mick, no furniture. Everything was gone. Everything was just black.

Then he saw her. His mother. Standing next to Asmodeus. Both his parents, here and now. Asmodeus reached for Jophiel's hand, and she took it. Fingers intertwined. They were truly in a forbidden love. She was beautiful, radiant, and so pure. He was a demon.

"How can this be?"

"Son, the book I gave you. It contains secrets that only demons possess. I know you learned more at the Town Hall than you mentioned to anyone. Edward told me what you learned. But listen to your mother. She has part of the knowledge you need that wasn't gained that day."

Jophiel smiled. Sully couldn't help but be in awe at her beauty and total pureness.

"A battle has waged between Heaven and Hell since the beginning of time. The Church knows it and therefore asks demon hunters like you to do what they cannot do in the most dire of times. But demon hunters can only be half-breeds to be successful by the Church's standards. It was a way to keep the balance in check. You are a half-breed, but not in the normal sense. You are one of a kind, as no other demon and no other angel have ever produced a child. The fate of the world relies on you doing what you will do. The archangel Michael suggested to both God and Lucifer that a child would be created, in part from each kingdom, and its destiny would be to keep the balance between Heaven and Hell on earth. It was permitted that Asmodeus and I get to know each other, hoping we would sire the chosen offspring. We did, but we also fell in love. We weren't supposed to fall in love. We created the child. You. Your great destiny is just unraveling for you because as Asmodeus learned, there are other demons that do not want the balance to be kept. Earth is the battlefield, and the annihilation of humans is the price. These demons… Asmodeus— help me if I need it."

She paused for a moment but then continued. "Sully, we know you don't trust demons, especially your father, but you are going to have to. There is no other choice. There are demons that are out to conquer the earth and gain entry back into Heaven. That cannot happen. There is a way. Through a key.

The key can open the gateway to either kingdom. Asmodeus also shared news about the organization that has been in touch with you. The Church does not include them. They say that, but it is not God's church they serve. They are the faction demons. The archangel Michael created a beacon that is the way to finding the key. You will know this beacon because she bears his mark. She is his daughter. You have the beacon. You must protect her. She will guide you to the key."

Sully looked at his parents in disbelief. Mick, the beacon? Him, the child of both kingdoms? His life was now taking another turn, but was it for the right purpose? He needed to find out.

"How will I find this key? There's only one like me? There are a lot of questions. I feel like a child. I need time. Time away from… from you both. But I will choose my path. I will protect Mick, if she is the one you speak of. But then, I must honor my promise to her. To save the bartender."

Sully closed his eyes again and used every ounce of strength he had to fight against his father's command of that one word. He returned and saw Mick lying there. Running to her side, he lifted her in his arms and laid her on the bed. Moving strands of hair away from her face, he fought the urge to just kiss her. He knew he would be clumsy at it, but he wanted to feel her lips again. Mick moved.

CHAPTER 15

Before Sully could help Mick up and finish explaining the situation, the apartment's door flew open, and there stood Margaret. And her crew.

Sully didn't have a minute to react before he heard Edward screaming as if he was in pain. It took him no more than a minute to realize that Edward was hit with a stun gun. Edward appeared to look all right, just in shock and pain. Sully could not count on him for the moment. There wasn't even time to reach for a weapon, but he didn't need one. Something inside him snapped. He drew his arms together so that they touched and the tattoos on the inner arms glowed red.

Sully, without thinking, screamed the only thing he could: "Redi ad inferos!" Margaret laughed at him.

Seconds later, the men that were around her vanished. He assumed they were demons, which made Margaret's alliance with them a little more interesting. Before they vanished, he noticed they were almost a match for the demons that took the bartender. Margaret lunged at him, reaching for his waist, hoping to use gravity and her weight to overpower him. Quick as can be, he found his blade and cut a small slice of skin that resulted in her screaming. Edward was no longer screaming, but Mick was. She had been shot with a stun gun as well. Mick lay on the ground, screaming in pain. That was two down for his side. Finally, he saw Edward rise and make his way toward Mick.

As Margaret arched her arm to give him a nice right hook, he leaned backward, missing the connection completely. But that didn't stop him from reaching for her, grabbing her wrists, and twisting them enough to force her to her knees. He looked down at her, tightening his grip. He had never once been violent against women, so he was careful as he asked Edward to find something to tie her wrists together. Edward came back with zip ties, while Mick stopped screaming.

"Ok, Margaret. Let's get on with it. You don't want me to help you with the Church or to learn about your organization. You want me for some other purpose. What do you want?"

Margaret remained silent. And defiant.

Sully used his own language on her. "Teine."

The fire appeared in front of her and heat rose from the flames. He could see Margaret trying to scoot back a little, so that her clothes would not touch the orange-red flames. Sully took a small breath and blew toward the fire, causing it to spread its heat toward his new prisoner.

"I can do this all day. We can do this the easy way or the hard way. Easy or hard. Your choice."

Margaret remained defiant. Mick somehow must have regained control of her fears because Sully saw her coming towards them. She stared at Margaret for a few minutes, always cocking her head to the left, then to the right. Sully wondered if Mick recognized her. He was wrong.

Mick said, "You are not a loyal servant of either Heaven or Hell. You want something. The key? But the key isn't here."

Then Mick fainted, and Sully caught her before she hit the floor. He didn't have time for these shit games. Sully had to embrace his true nature, his true destiny if he wanted answers. He knew his mother was right. Sully took some deep breaths, in and out. In and out again. Then, he relaxed his shoulders and let the truth of who he was flow through his body, through his mind. He was the demon hunter, the son of a demon *and* an archangel. He was... the child of Heaven and Hell. As he took his last breath, his body changed.

He felt a power, unlike anything he had ever felt before, flow through him. His shoulder blades burned, and then he felt them. Wings growing out of his body. Symbols appeared all over, looking like he had gotten a full body of artwork tattooed on his skin. He let out a scream that shook the walls. Sully was not the same person as he was an hour ago. He was much, much more.

He took the time to look at Margaret. He studied her eyes.

"It's true. You are the one we need. Sully, I can help you. You must believe me."

"Believe you? I think not. But I want more answers about this organization. Does the organization have the bartender? Is that why you planned to meet me? To take an innocent human for your purposes?"

Margaret just stared at him. "Foolish demon hunter. We don't have him. We don't need him. It is you we want. And now, you led me to her. She isn't on my list, but who is she? She's obviously powerful. Join us and we can enter both Heaven and Hell together. We can give you the answers to your past that you always wanted."

Sully didn't believe her. Instead, he placed his hands on her shoulder. "Go back to your organization now. If you ever come back here, I will destroy you. I am giving you the chance to leave and tell them I am not like you. Leave me alone."

He didn't untie Margaret but showed her the door. He let her go away on her own and he didn't care. He watched as Margaret disappeared down the hall. Hopefully for good.

As he faced Edward, he smiled and said, "I know who I am now."

Edward returned the smile as Sully went to take care of Mick. He raised her head and tried to bring her around. It was no use. She mumbled a bunch of unique phrases in the angel's language. She knew Enochian. But he could understand her too! This must be what his mother meant when she spoke to him before. He listened to her phrases.

"To find the key, visit the two mountains near the place where the first garden is believed to be… the secret is within the key… the hour of darkness and light will merge when the sun and moon touch…"

More riddles, but this was something Sully was good at, given his nature. But first, Mick had to wake up. He cradled her head and smoothed out her hair. She looked peaceful and beautiful in this state. The mumbling stopped. Her eyes suddenly opened, and Mick spoke in the same language as before. She said that they had to leave as the destroyer was coming for them. Sully didn't know whom she was referring to, but then realized it had to be Abaddon. The destroyer. Shit. The world was going to hell in a handbasket, figuratively.

Before Sully could help Mick any further, the door flew open again. He'd just gotten rid of Margaret and now he has another problem to deal with.

"Demon hunter. Son of Asmodeus."

"Destroyer. Abaddon."

"I came for the girl. Don't interfere in things you know nothing about."

Sully stood. At his height, he knew he could overpower any demon, and, with his sheer strength, he never worried about losing. Until now. Abaddon was a force to be reckoned with. She was beautiful but sinful. After all, she was the destroyer. He noticed she glanced at Edward, but he disappeared. Probably in fear of her. Even he was trembling on the inside. Abaddon wore all black leather, her body slender and toned. To the average human, she was beautiful, but he knew that to be a façade. Being the hunter of demons, he could see her true physical appearance.

"Tell you what, destroyer. Come and dance with me. I'm not the same hunter you have heard of. Things changed for me. In fact, come look at what's on my finger." He raised his hand so she could see the ring on his finger.

"I am the heir. I acknowledge my father. Therefore, I inherited my true powers and more. So, I say again, demon, dance with me."

With that, he held out his hand as if he truly meant to dance with her. He meant to dance with her, but in his style. She came at him, but he dodged a blow she threw. This time, he took out the blade his father had given him. He waved it in front of her, teasing her almost. The blade shone in the light, and before his eyes, symbols appeared that marked his heritage. They connected with the symbols that were on the blade. His true nature. Abaddon stared at the blade and trembled, though she looked like she was trying to hide her fear.

"Dance with me, destroyer. Or would you rather feel the sharpness of my blade?"

He noticed Abaddon was staring at his blade. Sully chided himself. This is when they all did the same thing—wondered if they would survive their fight against him. It was always the same, but something told him that this was a tad different.

Before, he hadn't really accepted his true nature because he didn't know of his mother's side. The blade continued to glow in front of her as if it was talking to her about its power. Her eyes changed. She became fearful. Sully knew that look. As he tried to jab the blade towards her, she regained her composure and from her hands, a light flashed, and he was thrown back against the wall on the other side of the room. The world around him became black.

He opened his eyes and looked at the room. He was the only one there. Edward was gone. Mick was gone. He never felt so alone as he did now. Sully closed his eyes once more and hoped that all was a dream. Reopening his eyes, nothing had changed. He was still alone. Sully yelled for Edward.

Edward was at his side.

CHAPTER 16

Still reeling from the attack from Abaddon, Sully was more than pissed. He lost Mick. Not just a client, but a friend and, if what Asmodeus and Jophiel told him, she was to be his ally. Slamming his fist against the wall, he shook off his anger and told Edward that they needed to regroup. He must figure out this prophecy, form a plan, and go after Abaddon. He was going to need help.

Damn. The only person he could think of was Asmodeus, especially if he was going to avoid Margaret at all costs. The idea toyed with him but was dismissed given her allegiance.

Hours later, Sully gathered his strength with Edward's help. The two had become close over the last several weeks. More than ever before. It was time. For some inexplainable reason, he could determine the limits of his full power, as demon hunter and the son of both a demon and an archangel. But he knew the latter must be a closely guarded secret. He tapped into his powers with such ease that it even scared him a little.

Sully laid out all the books he'd collected over the years, what was given to him by Asmodeus and what he took from Scotland through the parchments. He stared at them with an intensity that must've alarmed Edward because Edward spoke, causing his mind to be interrupted.

"Brother, what are you doing? Shouldn't we be focused on staying hidden from the destroyer? Or finding Mick if we will not hide our demon asses."

Sully laughed as he ran his fingers through his hair, and that's when he felt something odd with his shoulders again. He never gave it a second thought regarding the pain because it came and went. And well, he had been a little distracted. Feeling beaten and still unsure of his new transformation, Sully called on the one he thought could help him by answering the questions he wanted to ask. Jophiel.

Kneeling and bowing his head in prayer, he simply said her name. Standing before him, Jophiel looked radiant. She was full of a heavenly glow that one could only imagine when thinking of angels.

"Let me get this straight. I've been 'created' by both Heaven and Hell for a purpose. Is that right? And that purpose is to protect the beacon and the key in order to prevent anyone or anything from entering both Heaven and Hell, leading up to an annihilation of the world. Mick seems to be the beacon. So, not only do I have to save her from the destroyer Abaddon, but I need to find her bartender friend, whom the demons have taken. And avoid this organization of faction demons. Is that my destiny?"

Jophiel smiled.

"You are my son. And you are the son of Asmodeus. Michael wanted a child between us placed on earth to protect the humans and both angels and demons. You've been a demon hunter for far too long. Demons were once angels, now fallen angels and welcomed into the kingdom of Hell. God chose not to have either kingdom harmed and therefore agreed to the idea and Satan. You are the chosen protector. Mick is more than just a beacon. She will discover that in time, it is not my place or story to tell. You've embraced both sides of your power, I can see that. You are now more powerful than ever before. But now, you need to balance both your demon side and your heavenly side. You are now half demon, half angel. Demon hunting is not your only obligation now. You can kill both demons and angels. But you can't choose one side over the other. To do that would cause annihilation to the world."

Sully tried to absorb what he heard, but then he showed her his newest tattoos. These had just appeared on him at some point. He showed her one in particular. It was a protection symbol, that much was clear to him, but it was unlike any other protection symbol he had used before or what was tattooed on him. This one had what looked like to be a powerful angelic-like sword in the middle of the symbol.

Jophiel stared at the symbol and smiled at him.

"Son, that is the highest mark of the holiest protection one can bear. This is the protection of God. It's marked that way because that is Michael's sword, the sword given to him by God. No harm can come to you. You are untouchable."

Sully laughed. "Well, Abaddon sure kicked my ass. There was harm."

"Not. She may throw you, or attack you, but your body will learn to absorb the powers of the demons that attack you and you can use it against them. You need to develop both sides to be whole. The Lord God will watch over you."

And with that, she disappeared just as easily as she came.

Now he did the next thing. He called for Asmodeus. He hoped this encounter would add to his new knowledge about his true self and what he needs to do and not another series of riddles. But before Asmodeus appeared, Sully hunched over, screaming in pain. The soul eater was making his presence known.

"What do you want, soul eater? We are supposed to coexist so that you can feed on my soul."

"Demon hunter, I remember the deal exactly. But you need me to save the girl that somehow holds your heart. You can't fool me."

Sully sighed. He closed his eyes and allowed the soul eater to share control of his body and mind. This time was different. They were both in control in the strangest of ways.

"Asmodeus. Come to me," he said once more. This time, Asmodeus appeared.

His father looked at him with a stare that shook his being. He couldn't figure out what he was doing until his father spoke.

"Soul eater. Son. You are one? Very curious thing you have done, my boy."

"I had no time, and he was inside me, not by my choice. So, I played it to my advantage. But you somehow knew, didn't you? Doesn't matter. I need to find Mick, but to save her, I need to know everything you can tell me about Abaddon. She took her. Then, I will rescue the bartender. I'm still figuring out the other stuff you and Jophiel told me."

"Son, you need to stop saying her name. For the sake of your soul and life."

"I'm already damned. But I know. I know. The balance must be kept. Tell me about these new powers I have. I need to tap into them."

Inside, Sully could feel the soul eater just drooling with anticipation to use his new powers. He didn't like it, but a deal was a deal. The soul eater was told to relax and let things happen. He knew they must work together. But the eagerness of the soul eater was too much for him to control.

"Asmodeus. Prince of Hell. You didn't tell him about all his powers, did you? I can feel them. He's a strong one, and he doesn't realize it yet. If you don't tell him, Abaddon will use his bones to tenderize his flesh, his organs to feed her minions. I can sense the other side, too. All powerful and he'll be dead before long if you don't teach him. Her—I can understand why she wouldn't show him but you? He can still be killed until he masters all his power." Sully was chuckling, but he knew it was because of the soul eater.

"In order to tap into your powers, you need to come to Hell. You can return, but you need to embrace the place where your powers come from. There is no other way."

"Is this the only way to get Mick back? And the bartender?"

Asmodeus lowered his head and nodded. Sully thought for a moment that his father didn't enjoy presenting the idea to him and never wanted his son to see Hell, but, if it is the only way, so be it. He couldn't get Mick out of his mind. It was like torture for him. But he returned the nod in agreement.

"You won't need your vials but bring the book I gave you. That can't leave your side. Let's go now."

Before Sully could get Edward, Asmodeus had already sent him to Hell.

CHAPTER 17

Hell was not like he expected it, but then again, Sully never gave Hell or Heaven a lot of thought. Asmodeus took him on a brief tour, but he realized that the demons in Hell stared at him once they noticed his ring. He was feeling self-conscious, but the soul eater lent him the courage he lacked. His mind kept wandering to the thought of Mick, the kiss, her soft skin, until the soul eater shook him back to reality.

He saw demon after demon bowing as he walked by. He just stared at them, knowing that he could kill them in a heartbeat. What was it his mother had said? He must balance both sides. Damn. Demon hunting was all he knew.

Asmodeus brought him to a chamber where a poor, unfortunate soul was being tortured. He could feel the soul eater enjoying the sight of this. The tunnels all looked the same as they walked into the chamber. But this chamber was dark, almost giving him an eerie feeling.

"What is this room?"

Asmodeus laughed. "This is my place of fun. Well, torture to some but fun for me. I'm a demon."

Sully couldn't shake the man's screams from his thoughts.

"Here is where the training begins."

Sully spent the next several hours in the training room. Well, he guessed hours, learning his skills, his abilities, the meaning behind his tattoos. His body survived the heat of Hell, but not the screams. The tortured souls were getting to him and finally, he had enough. He wanted to return after learning more about his new abilities, but Asmodeus wouldn't let him go just yet. He was getting annoyed.

"Father or not, let me return. I will find Mick with what you showed me. I can't maintain my destiny of balance if I stay here too long. Let me go."

Asmodeus just smiled and laughed. "You didn't learn everything you need to yet. I need you to learn our ways. I think I will have you torture those whose screams you can't stand. Learn that and we will talk about your freedom."

Sully refused. That would go against every fiber in his being, his vow to God. But, then again, hadn't he already broken his vows by kissing Mick? Reluctantly, he agreed, though he knew the screams would make it hard for him to complete the task. But the soul eater reassured him.

"Your father does not know of our agreement. Take a mental nap or something, and I will endure the task at hand. But do not trust anyone here in Hell, including Asmodeus. I serve the master of Hell, not your father. Something is off here. I smell betrayal. At least with Lucifer, I know where I stand. Something isn't right."

Sully, not sure who to trust anymore, placed his trust in the soul eater. The soul eater needed him; he needed the soul eater. What had he called it again? The unholy alliance. Sully went to "sleep" and the soul eater completely took over. The soul eater made sure that Asmodeus was none the wiser, and he began the task against the tortured souls. As the souls were tortured in the most hideous ways, the soul eater was enjoying every minute of it, but as much as he wanted to feed on the souls, he didn't. Time went by in Hell.

In the end, Asmodeus was quite impressed with the task performed. But Sully was still not free. More tasks upon more tasks were placed on him and the soul eater performed them while Sully was in his mental nap with the soul eater in charge. A sultry woman was approaching him, and the soul eater woke him up.

"Demon hunter, switch with me. She is coming and your father can't know what we've done."

Sully was now in control and didn't have time to gather his wits before she ran her hands up and down his torso. He was uncomfortable but didn't respond to show it. He needed to figure out what had happened, but first fend her off. She was a demon, but beautiful as well.

"Demon hunter, you finally came down here," she said in a raspy voice as her fingers twirled her hair. Her tongue gave him a little flick in the most sensual way.

He looked at her. Those lips, her eyes, her voice. Intoxicating. She ran her hands all over him, and was quite forceful in her grip, just tight enough to arouse him. Sully tried to stop her, but she threw him against the wall and pushed him onto the floor. She crawled her way on top of him with her face stopping right at his belt. Her hands were toying with his belt while she was breathing slightly heavy.

"Who the hell are you?"

"I'm whomever you want me to be. Do you want me to be her? Or do you want me to be him?" Slowly, her hands moved to undo his belt buckle, while her tongue moved around her lips in the most tempting of ways. Her eyes never left his. Her body shifted slowly to the left and right, enticing him even more.

"Why do I feel that you're toying with me, demon?"

"Would you prefer me to be your nightmare or your fantasy?"

She lifted his shirt, exposing his abs. She kissed his stomach in so many places and in the sexiest of ways. He could feel her fingernails lightly scratch against his skin. His mind did not recall the vows he made before, nor did he recall the thought of Mick or the bartender.

He was enjoying the moment. His body was responding to her. He tried to pull her face close to his to kiss her. Finally, his lips met hers.

"Why are you doing this? I'm… I'm the son of Asmodeus."

"Oh, demon hunter, you are much more than that, and you know it. I know who you really are. I am so curious about you."

Before she could finish, Sully was lost in her trance. But the soul eater was not. The soul eater fought for control and won over him. Through his eyes, the soul eater stared at the demon. His eyes pierced into her, and she must've recognized him because she whispered, "Soul eater."

He just laughed at her and pulled her closer to him, kissing her back with such intensity that she wiggled out of his grasp. She couldn't break free. But his hands only tightened their grasp and as he held onto her tightly, his body still was responding to her. He was aroused. She tried to hold the soul eater down with her legs and he felt the power in her ankles, but he took his legs and spread them, causing her legs to separate while she remained on top of him.

"Tell me why."

The demon smiled and said, "Asmodeus commanded me to make it impossible for the demon hunter to leave Hell. I will be rewarded if I succeed. He wants his son here. Mortals cringe, angels fall from Heaven and demons rise from Hell."

"Foolish demon. He is just a half-breed."

"He is more. He is a bad, bad boy, son of the demon of lust. Every little girl's dream come true, and he was promised to me by Asmodeus himself. You deny his order?"

Laughing, the soul eater said, "Asmodeus doesn't scare me. You know who I serve unless you want to serve the demon hunter. Go against the demon of lust and side with his son. That's where the true power lies, and Asmodeus knows it."

The soul eater called Sully to join him. There was no time to lose. Sully and the soul eater were now one more than before. There would be no back and forth for control of his body. Sully and the soul eater completely merged into one.

Sully pushed her hands back and tried to get her off him. He realized the facade immediately once they merged. He could not stay in Hell any longer.

"Deny me if you can. But it is you who will keep me inside you, longing and wanting."

She slowly crawled back off him. Sully was free of her and watched her scurry away, like a woman in Los Angeles who does the nightly walk of shame. Standing up, he fixed himself and silently thanked the soul eater. He felt different, somehow, but there was no time to figure out what it was exactly. Sully just knew that there was something physically different about him, but he didn't know how or what.

Taking a deep breath, he prepared to yell in his loudest voice, "ASMODEUS! You will come to your son, NOW! FATHER."

Asmodeus appeared in front of him and gave him a knowing look.

"Ah, you and the soul eater. Somehow, the alpha in you came out. Do not summon me like you are the prince of Hell, because you are not, boy. Not yet. You are just my heir. What do you want?"

"You can't keep me here. Set me free. You know what I need to do. You and Jophiel said so." His voice echoed through the walls of Hell, causing them to shake. Sully was taken aback by his power and stared at his father, who looked slightly afraid.

Asmodeus shrugged. "I just wanted you here with me. You didn't need me until recently, no matter how many times I made Edward try to persuade you. I will release you, but you will come back to me. You can't stay away forever. Especially since you tasted her kiss just now. Your power is amplified. You are so much more. Neither your mother nor I knew what your full potential could be. The agreement never spoke of such intense power. You must be careful, my son. You will need Edward. He is not much to look at, but even you don't realize his potential because you were never ready to accept him or your rightful place till now. Soul eater, listen closely. Any harm to my son and I will hunt you. I will have Lucifer hunt you down. My son doesn't know the danger that will come for him once they know his real nature."

Sully clenched his fists together and fought the anger inside him, thinking of his mother. A sense of calm filled him. What a family. Family ties that bind.

As one, he knew Hell completely. He knew the way out and he could only assume it was because of the merge with the soul eater. Sully left Hell and didn't look back.

CHAPTER 18

Sully and Edward were walking the streets of Los Angeles, and something felt off to him. As he walked past a convenience store, he got the sense that people were acting differently. Backing up, he walked into the store and found a newspaper on the counter. The cashier told him it was his, so Sully asked, "Can I just see this for a moment?" The cashier nodded.

Grabbing the paper, he looked at the date. It was nearly three months later since he was taken to Hell. Edward explained that time works slower in Hell and with him having been down there, he wasn't sure what all could've happened. Sully was in the mood for a drink and went to the beer section but was stopped by the familiar smell of demons. Turning around slowly, he prepared his body by cocking his head to the left and then to the right while flexing his arms. His tattoos turned red, something they had never done before.

"Demon hunter."

"I'm sorry, do I know you?" He thought to play coy with them. Why not have a little fun?

The demons moved around him, forming a circle. Sully was a man of instinct. In his head, he was already figuring out the easiest path out of the store without causing a lot of chaos. Hopefully, the demons wouldn't make too much of a mess. These demons didn't look familiar to him, but he knew they wanted something from him.

"We want the key."

"My house key? My car key? Wait, I don't have a car. Looks like I can't help you, fellas."

The first demon, the biggest of them all, stepped forward, readied both hands and clenched them into fists. He tried to take a swing at Sully, but he leaned back and missed the connection. Being quick on his feet, he dropped and swept his leg around to knock the demon on his back. The other two pinned his arms back and waited for the fallen demon to get up.

"Hold the hunter." They did. The leader punched Sully a few times, and he took it.

Sully let his head hang down, appearing to look defeated. In his head, he counted the seconds and watch the demon's feet moving toward him. One, two, three… As soon as the demon was close enough, Sully took a breath and kicked out his right leg, meeting the demon's abdomen. As the demon staggered backward, he then flexed his arms and moved them forward, forcing the other two to lose their grip on him, changing their stances. He punched the one on the right and turned to kick the other one. After a little more "fun," all three demons were on the ground. He went to the leader and took out his knife. Stepping over him, he held his knife at his throat, demanding that the others back down. Which they did.

"Who sent you? Was it Abaddon? Margaret? Who do you serve, damnit?"

"I'm not telling you, hunter. We'll see you in Hell soon."

Before Sully could ask another question, all the demons vanished as quickly as they had arrived. Sully slammed his fist against the floor to relieve himself of his anger. He was still angry. The cashier came running towards him and started yelling about the mess. Sully shrugged and, knowing he couldn't just walk out of there without helping, so he cleaned up the store first. The cashier mumbled his thanks and told him to never come back.

Sully and Edward returned to his apartment and found that they were not alone. Abaddon. The place was trashed, and Sully motioned for Edward to search the rooms to ensure that nothing was missing. Edward obeyed. He also knew that with Edward occupied, he and Abaddon could have a long overdue talk.

"You."

Abaddon just laughed at his feeble word. She walked towards him, blowing him a kiss using her red, pouty lips.

Dressed all in black, she looked good. Sully shook his head to get such thoughts out of his mind. He couldn't make sense of all these thoughts because for so long, he never gave the other sex a second thought in that way. Then he realized with his awakened abilities and his acceptance of being the son of the Demon of Lust, he must have triggered his true nature from Asmodeus. She slowed her approach towards him, stopping just briefly in front of him. Her gloved hand stroked the side of his face gently until she gave him a fierce slap.

The slap, having shaken him, caused his arm to reach up and grab her wrist as she tried to do it again for fun. Clasping her hand so she couldn't break his grip, he simply commanded her, "Drop." He drew on all his power to say that one word and Abaddon fell to her knees.

"I'm the destroyer. How dare you try to control me? Your little girlfriend is fine. She's my new plaything."

"Where is she? She has no part in this. You know that. I am the one you want. It is my destiny to protect the key and you won't reach the key."

Abaddon broke free from his control and stood up, looking him straight in the eye. His patience was running out. He had to find Mick. Sully watched her closely. Abaddon knew something. That much was clear with the way she eyed him up and down. He showed her the tattoo of protection, the one Jophiel told him about. He brought his arm closer to her so that she could get a closeup of who he truly was. Her eyes changed. She started screaming at him.

"Why do you want your girlfriend, hunter? Do you know her real identity? She showed her true colors while I tortured her in Hell. Don't worry, she still breathes. For now. But for how long is up to you? Give me that key and you can have her. Even exchange, hunter."

Sully raised his arms, exposing both palms outward to her. "You want to see what I truly am? What I am capable of, destroyer?"

Taking a calming breath, he focused his mind on his shoulder blades. He knew that along with his birthright, came the one thing that made his transcendence complete. His wings. Focusing on his shoulder blades, he summoned his wings to emerge from the little nubs that recently appeared. Once he could feel his wings spread, he looked to the wall where the light reflected his shadow. From empowerment to fear. He didn't have to kill her, he just had to scare her. Then he noticed Abaddon's face had changed. Using that same commanding voice as before, he commanded her back to her knees. Calling to Edward that all was safe, he waited for him to appear.

"Listen, destroyer of all, I accepted my place and my birthright. I am the son of Asmodeus, Prince Demon of Lust." Pausing, he contemplated if he should just spill the rest. "And I am the son of Jophiel, one of the highest angels of the kingdom of Heaven. I hold the power to kill both demons and angels. The power to let both live is mine. I am untouchable. I will find Mick. You can warn the others that I know who I am and what I am capable of. You can either return her to me or I will barge into Hell or whatever shithole of a place you are keeping her and kill everyone I see to save her. As far as the key that opens the passage to Heaven and Hell, I have it in my possession. You can't get it because you can't kill me."

He hoped the little lie about the key would be something she believed because he didn't have any other card to play now. Sully also hoped he was right that nothing could kill him now. He wanted her to know who he was, and that he accepted his rightful place. Finally. After all these centuries, he acknowledged what he'd known all along—he was the heir to his father's domain in Hell. He was the son of Asmodeus. Sully was afraid to think too much of Jophiel and lose his advantage over Abaddon.

Edward stepped closer. He felt a sense of power from his brother, giving him more strength over her. Sully thought Abaddon showed a small sign of fear, but he could be wrong because she quickly advanced towards him. Touching Edward on the shoulder caused his wings to send fire to her hands. Abaddon screamed before leaving. His father was right about Edward being advantageous for him.

"Brother, you look different. You don't look like you anymore."

Sully ran to the bathroom mirror and screamed. His once dark hair was now dark on the bottom and blue on top. He ran his fingers through his hair, which felt the same but was longer on the top than the bottom. Blue strands hung towards his cheeks. His eyes were different, but he knew he was still the same person. His scars were gone, and he removed his shirt to see what other changes had taken place.

His body was literally covered in ancient symbols, representing both Heaven and Hell. He turned to see his back in the mirror. That's when he noticed it. His wings. Though he could collapse and extract them as needed, one wing was gold, while the other was black. Sully remembered his mother's word. Balance. He noticed the large symbol in the middle of his back. The symbol of something both pure and evil. The words on the bottom of the symbol were in both languages. It read, "This is the agreement between two kingdoms. He is the protector and the destroyer." As he examined his body, there was no turning back now. But perhaps he had what he needed to rescue Mick. And then to save the bartender.

Sully was still in awe of his transformation. It was as if he was unrecognizable to himself. He'd always prided himself on his Scottish looks when he told people he was from Scotland. It was more acceptable to society than saying he was from Heaven and Hell. He looked in the mirror once more. His pupils were green with the iris also green, his brows had a small separation in the hair on each one and his jawline was now more pronounced. The body was bulkier and stronger. Sully kept turning around to eye himself until Edward got his attention.

Edward stood behind him and tried to reassure him. "You're not ugly, brother. I like the blue hair. It's different. It's longer too. Nice."

"It is. I look different, but I kind of like it. Aye!"

Sully noticed that for as long as he tried to fit in and hide his real identity, this was a twist. For a while, he continued to admire his new looks in the mirror. He felt stronger, better, and maybe a little more on the bad side.

Edward suggested a few additional changes and before long, Sully was ready to find Mick.

CHAPTER 19

Sully knew of an old, abandoned building in the darkest part of Los Angeles. It was used by various demons for sinister purposes, or just to hide from hunters like him. He knew the building well because this was an easy killing field for him. He prepared for his hunt by changing into black jeans, a black shirt and he carried his sword across his back, blades in his boots and pockets. He'd brought out his satchel since the book was now part of his attire. Carrying the book everywhere was going to be a challenge, but perhaps it would aid him. He hoped the building would hold a clue where to find Mick given the demons were always using it for things. His instinct also told him to check it out, but he had to wait till nightfall. Demons usually were active at night in order to stay hidden from humans.

"Not bad, hunter. We look damn good if I don't say so myself. Good enough to kill demons or angels."

"We are hunting demons. Not angels today. The aim is to save Mick. I'm talking to myself. Shit, people are going to think I'm insane."

"Hunter, we can communicate through our mind. We are one now, not two."

Edward called Sully to move along. "Brother, hurry. I want to see your new powers."

Sully shrugged and finished getting ready. His stomach growled, so he knew he needed to eat soon. He figured they would stop to eat. Never kill a demon on an empty stomach. After eating, Sully and Edward continued their journey to the building. As soon as they got closer to it, Edward reached for Sully's hand. Despite his child-like size, it was hard to remember that he was nearly the same age as Sully. He took his hand and reassured him. The building was impressive, even though it was falling apart on the outside. Demons lay on the ground all around them. Some were oblivious to his approach.

Sully walked over demons, and before, he would have just killed them. But remembering the balance, he let them be. They didn't care that he was there. A group of demons emerged from the shadows and captured Edward.

"Damn."

Edward was resisting the best he could, but it was no use. The demons held onto him and goaded Sully into a fight. Sully felt intense heat from within and realized that the soul eater was lending its strength and power to him. With that power plus his newfound powers, there was no telling what he was capable of. He needed to find out what his strengths were. He spoke to the demons.

"Let him go. You don't want him. You want the son of Asmodeus, don't you? I'm not afraid. Come get me."

From behind the demons emerged another. It was her. Sully could only say one word.

"Shit."

It was the demon woman from Hell that wanted him earlier. He had to be stronger. He had to resist her. Looking at her, his body heated with an intense drive. His heart was pounding faster and his breath was becoming shallower. This had to be her in control.

She laughed as she came closer to him. Her hand ran through his hair.

"Demon hunter, you changed your hair. I like it. You are different now. Why is that?"

Sully inhaled, then exhaled to show restraint. He didn't have any. Then he remembered that he and the soul eater were one. He grabbed her by the waist and pulled her closer to him. Sully moved his hand to the center of her back. He then moved to act like he was dipping her in a dance and breathed his words in her ear.

"I am not the same hunter you met before, demon. I am so much more now. And you know what the best part is, you little demon whore?" Sully didn't wait for a response before speaking again. "I am not *just* a demon hunter. I am the son of a demon and an angel. You can't kill me, but if you'd like to try, I'll let you."

And with that, he brought her back upright and stared straight into her eyes. "Do you want to dance with me?"

She must've been furious because instead of trying to kiss, she launched a full assault on him. Sully took her punches, recalling what his mother said. He had the power to absorb their strengths or something like that. Seeing that she was cupping her hands to attack him, he steadied himself, preparing to receive the blow. Once the blow hit him, he reeled back a few steps, but he was still standing. His body absorbed the fire that she threw at him. She threw more at him. He just continued to absorb it.

Having enough of this game, Sully reached for his sword and swung it at her. It did not miss. Where she once stood was now a pile of ashes. Looking at the other demons, he smiled. "Who's next?" The demons let Edward go.

"Damn brother! You're a force to be feared. I wonder if God and Lucifer knew what you'd be capable of when they agreed."

Ignoring what Edward said, he spoke. "Edward, are you ok? We must find Mick. I don't know where she is. Let's go."

Sully listened to Edward, trying to back out of the plan, but he understood. He wasn't much of a fighter. He did his best to reassure Edward. They walked the halls, searching room to room. He gagged when he came across one room. It wasn't what he expected at all. Sully found the missing bartender. He was hung upside down and spread as if he were on a crucifix. Blood was dripping down his body, and the smell was haunting and foul.

Sully coughed a few times before the coughs became deeper. He had to check if he was still alive. He recognized him from the illusion in his apartment. Sully approached the body and knelt to look at his face. Placing his finger under the man's nose, he felt the faintest of breaths. He stood and hurried to take him down. He must've lost a lot of blood. Motioning for Edward to be quiet, he bent closer to the man's nose and mouth.

"I wouldn't tell them the prophecy. Save Mick. You must...save...her."

And with that last word, the bartender convulsed before dying. Years of practice gave Sully the knowledge to treat the wounded. He wondered if he could resurrect a life. The life of an innocent. He was half an angel. The more he thought about it, the more he concentrated on it.

He placed his hands on the man's chest and said a prayer. A prayer taught to him long ago by his abbot, though he never understood what it meant till now. As he prayed, he vowed to both God and Lucifer to maintain the balance and power placed on him to protect angels, demons, and innocents. Inside him, the soul eater agreed as well to the promise Sully made. A light filled the room. Sully was blinded for a moment. He checked the man once more. The man was breathing.

Sully experienced a dizzy spell and nausea, so he sat on the floor. He thought it was because he was new to using these powers. The soul eater was also weakened now that they were one. He just couldn't get back up. Feeling Edward shake him still didn't bring his senses back. Sully slipped further away. Then he heard a voice. He knew that voice. It was Mick.

"You need to get up. Use your powers to find me."

Using all his power, Sully stood and shook off the weird feeling he was having. He communicated with the soul eater and together, they came up with a plan. She was here. Sully could feel her once he heeded her message. He tapped into his powers. Extending his wings, he was no longer hiding his identity. It was too late for that.

Sully made sure the bartender was alive and safe. The man also stood. Sully noticed the man staring at his wings. Placing his hands on the man's shoulder, he reassured him he would find Mick but that he must stay with him for his own safety. The bartender nodded, but not before asking Sully, "What are you?"

Sully smiled. "I am the protector of angels and demons. As well as humans. There is something about you that makes you unique. You..you can read the languages."

The man laughed. "I am the prophet. I am the one who hid the key you seek. At least I am not the one who has lived many lifetimes. Although my life would have ended if it hadn't been for you. The demons drained my energy and there was no hope of saving me. I am thankful you came along."

"Does Mick know what you are?"

"Call me Elias. For a long time, I've waited for you."

Sully sensed something was wrong. Or was it that Mick's message pressed in his mind, forcing him to hurry? They continued to search the rooms. They were near the last door. There was no time for games. Using his body weight, he forced his way into the room.

Mick was unconscious and laid on a table. Black candles surrounded her, and a demon stood over her. Sully noticed the demon was oblivious to his presence. He stood and watched the demon. Then he recognized the demon because of the soul eater's knowledge. It was Balam. Balam commanded over forty legions of demons and was one of the most powerful demons in Hell. He could turn men into anything. It wasn't good for Mick if he was the one behind taking her. Abaddon was only the tool to capture Mick.

Again, he worried about Edward's safety and motioned for him to crawl back. He noticed Elias stood in the back and remained solemn in his position. Sully extended his wings and held his sword in his hands. Strands of his blue hair hung over his face, hiding his eyes. The demon did not look up. The soul eater shared his knowledge of this demon with him. The demon wouldn't fear Sully.

But that could change.

Armed with his sword in one hand, the other he extended outward towards Balam. He didn't know what to do. Say a prayer, cast a curse? Sully was frustrated, but then he felt something change. His symbols were burning into his skin. Then he felt it. The power from Balam. Balam was one of those demon factions that he had been told about. Or was he the leader?

"Balam, I command you to unleash the girl from your power."

Balam stared at Sully and just laughed. "You command me? The king of demons? Nice try, boy."

Balam stopped hovering over Mick and moved towards Sully. Sully counted on the soul eater to help, as he didn't know what Balam was capable of. He counted three heads—a bull, a man's head, and a ram. This would not be pleasant.

Sully summoned forth his strength and prayed. As he had with saving Elias, he prayed to both sides. Sully spoke to the demon. He promised retribution against Balam for hurting Mick. Then he used his sword, which glowed in the dark room, and attacked.

The demon scurried back against the wall, but he wasn't defeated. The two continued their fight and Balam called for his minions. In the room that was once empty save Sully, Edward, Elias, Balam, and Mick, it was now overflowing with demons. Sully was surrounded. He felt defeated. But then Elias appeared next to him.

CHAPTER 20

Sully knew he couldn't protect Elias and Edward at the same time while fighting Balam's demons. It was too much. He wondered about some of his powers. Remembering what Asmodeus taught him in Hell, Sully called upon fire to burn the demons while unleashing a power that Asmodeus wasn't sure he had. Asmodeus told him that his mother had the power to create weapons. That would be used by the angels. Asmodeus also said that she was the angel of beauty and never a fighter. He wondered if he, too, could create a sword to handle all these demons in one move or several. Sully tapped into the powers of the soul eater along with his own.

The room was filled with a bright light thanks to the sword. This sword has protected him for centuries. His favorite and well used sword had killed thousands of demons. Sully had etched symbols in the hilt that would aid in the killing of demons. When he designed this sword, the blacksmith from a very long time ago, was so impressed with his artistic ability. The blacksmith did not realize what he was creating at the time. The black handle was easy to grip. And once more, the sword did not fail him. The demons disappeared. All but Balam. Sully used the fire once more and aimed it at the demon king himself. He must've gotten his attention because the two fought. Meanwhile, Elias moved closer to the table. Sully noticed he was trying to revive Mick, but it was no use. Mick appeared to be close to death. That was when Edward moved towards them, leaving Sully alone with Balam.

Balam came towards him, casting out blasts of fire over and over. Sully stood in his spot, lowered his sword, and absorbed the fire. His tattoos turned red, outlined with the color of gold. That's what got Balam's attention, or at least he thought.

"You? You're just a demon hunter. Nothing more. And I am the demon king."

It was Sully's turn to laugh. He removed his shirt and turned around, baring his back. Turning his head to the left, he looked over his shoulder. Sully couldn't resist the urge to show Balam the tattoo of the pact between Heaven and Hell. That's when he decided it was time to unleash the soul eater.

In a loud voice, he said, "Balam. I have another surprise. The soul eater and I are one. I possess the powers of both Heaven and Hell. And surprise, the power of the soul eater is mine as well. Do you wish to dance with me?" Sully realized he liked that phrase more and more for fighting demons.

Balam still showed no fear to Sully. This would not be easy. The two continued to clash and fight. Every fireball, everything that Balam threw at him, he only absorbed. Sully made a play.

"I can absorb your power, demon king. Continue trying if you dare. In fact, I insist. I will remain standing because of who I am. I am of both kingdoms. Your faction will recognize me now, demon king."

Balam stopped fighting him and looked as if he was thinking about his predicament. "Take the girl. I got what I wanted from her. I unlocked the secret of the key." That's when Sully noticed he looked at Elias.

"Isn't that right, prophet? You know where the key is. And I unlocked her secret. I will find the key and then I can enter Heaven anytime I please."

Sully tried to make a move against Balam, but as hard as he tried to return the fireballs, he couldn't. Somehow, his powers were not working. His strength was not there. Balam continued to taunt him, showing him who was in control. He raised both his hands, and Sully couldn't dodge the next blow.

"Shit. This is going to hurt."

Balam sent a blast towards Sully, powerful enough to knock him off his feet. He landed against the wall. Then he felt something from Mick. He tried to home in on it.

"Sully, I am more than the beacon. Save me. I am your shield. Use my power."

Sully shook off the effects of the attack and stood up. He made his way towards Mick, knowing that Balam could catch him off guard again. But it surprised him because Balam just let him go towards her. Was Balam giving in? He couldn't be sure.

Once Sully made his way to Mick, he reached for her hand. Clenching it in his hand, he could sense that she was merging her power with him. Now armed with the powers of his true nature, the soul eater, and now Mick, Sully was unstoppable. But so was Balam.

Sully raised his other hand and pointed it toward Balam. From his palm, a light materialized and aimed into the demon.

"Go back to hell." Sully sent the demon king back to Hell, knowing that it was only temporary.

Still holding onto Mick, Sully blew out the candles that surrounded her. With Elias's and Edward's help, he could free her, but she didn't wake. That's when Elias asked to help her. Sully nodded, appreciating the gesture. Elias breathed into his cupped hands and placed them on her forehead. After a few brief moments, he spoke. He left his hand on her forehead.

"She'll be alright. Her secret is still inside. Balam saw her secret but he didn't erase it. There's a reason she's the beacon, Sully. As the daughter of Michael, she knows where the key is. She will always know where the key is, even if it is ever lost. If we can find the key and get to it before Balam or any other demon gets it, then the passage is protected. We need to wake her, but she is very weak. What about your power?"

Sully still felt weak, but not as weak as before. She had lent him her power, and he thought about how to wake her. He placed his hand over Elias's and together, Sully could feel a touch of power flowing from him to her. Mick was moving and before long, her eyes fluttered open. Her dark eyes looked into his. In a voice that was deeper than hers, someone or something spoke through her.

"Child of both kingdoms. You have accepted your true destiny. Where you go, my daughter will go. Prophet, accompany them to find the key. Guard them as best you can. Take them to the first garden. But beware of both fallen angels and demons that will come for you."

Sully help Mick sit up, and while holding her, he instructed Edward to guard the door. He felt they would be safe in this room, but only for a moment. Soon, they would need to leave. Sully saw Edward was a little scared at what had just happened. He could tell based on how he just stared.

"Sully? You look different. Your hair is blue. I feel weak." And with that, Sully caught her as she fell back into his arms.

"Edward, it will be alright. She's weak. If you want to go back to father, I'll understand."

Edward shook his head. "No, brother. I am with you. I'm just not keen on the other side, but I was told to help you the best I can. Where you go, I go."

Elias put his hand on Sully's shoulder and gave it a squeeze.

"Demon hunter, we are a strange group but brought together to save two kingdoms. You will need us all at your side. You heard the voice of the archangel Michael."

Sully nodded. He turned to focus back on Mick, who seemed a little more alert than moments ago. Sully listened as she told him about what she learned about herself, the memories that were locked inside. She'd only discovered what or who she was when Balam had entered her mind.

***

"It was so strange, Sully. This woman or demon, whatever the fuck she was, took me to a place I've never seen before. It was dark and full of fire. She told me it was Hell and as I looked around, I realized that the picture books make it look nicer than it really is. Then she took me to another demon. The bastard was evil and brought me here. I could feel him enter my mind. It was so invasive. Sully…"

Mick broke down and began sobbing before she pulled herself together. She saw the look of worry in his eyes. He changed. He was good looking before but her mind couldn't help but think of her fantasies with him. Before he or the others could see what she was thinking, she continued but not before taking a deep breath and wiping her eyes.

"I saw images. People I've dreamed about but never really knew. He looks like an angel-tall, strong, and holy. He was holding a baby, but I knew it wasn't any of you. It was..me. God, that sounds so strange. This angel was protecting the baby from something, I guess, but he was talking to me. He told me not to worry because the protector was coming and I should help him. Tell him where to find me. I must be going crazy. Sully, can we get out of here? I'm scared and this place gives me the creeps."

Sully didn't respond but the next thing she knew, his arms were around her, in a tight hug. She had to tell him that she couldn't breathe but she also.

didn't want the embrace to end. Mick hugged him back but gently eased the embrace so that they could leave this awful place.

***

Once he felt she rested long enough, he told them all that they had to leave as soon as possible but to be on guard. He asked Edward and Elias to help Mick walk until she was strong enough. He wanted to lead the way to destroy anything that got in their way. Sully was not taking any chances with this group. Deep down, the soul eater agreed with him and once again, lent his strength and power to him. As far as alliances went, Sully was learning to appreciate this one.

The newly formed group made their way through the halls with ease. The demons that inhabited the building had no interest in them, as far as Sully could tell. But there was one that was after him for other reasons. He was going to have to get used to being the son of

Asmodeus, a demon of lust. It really was getting on his nerves, but now was not the time to deal with this issue.

Eventually, they made their way back to Sully's apartment, only to find a note on the door. Sully removed the knife to read the note.

> *Sully, you have one more chance to join us*
> *and let us teach you the secrets of the*
> *organization. I didn't leave town, hunter.*
> *Meet me in the bar of my hotel alone in two*
> *days. I have the parchments you left behind*
> *in Scotland.*
> *Margaret*

Crumpling the note, Sully noted he had no intention of including Margaret or her organization in any of his affairs. But something ate at him about the parchments. They contained a lot of information…but then he remembered he'd brought some of that information home with him. He just hoped it would be enough.

Once inside the apartment, the group huddled around the table with Sully, who showed them the information he had. Then it was time to listen to the prophet share his knowledge.

CHAPTER 21

Sully listened to Elias and noticed that Edward had fallen asleep. Mick was lost in thought, just staring out the window. Because she was still too weak. Sully noticed she had fallen asleep. However, he was intrigued that this mere bartender, a tall skinny fellow, was a prophet. He even wondered at his age. He noticed Elias was looking at him.

"You must be curious about me, hunter. What is it?"

Sully laughed out loud and said, "Elias, I was asked to find a bartender. Someone who never missed a day of work, who lives in a shabby-like apartment, and I come across you, almost dead but still breathing. And you are a prophet. So, why are you here?"

Elias put down the parchments he had in his hand, and said, "I was always here with Mick, in some form or another. My job was to always watch over her, being a friend and waiting till one day she would 'awaken' in her path. The day the demons took me, I was examining my books. I could decipher something that I hadn't been able to before. It was about the key. Well, it was more like a map. Before the demons came, I hid it in one book. I finished hiding it. I need to get back to my place to get it."

Sully smiled. "There's no need, friend. I took the books that I thought would bear fruit in my finding you. Look in them first and see if I brought the right ones unless you hid it somewhere else. But I will go with you if we have to go back there. Edward can watch after Mick. She will be safe here, given all my protection symbols and my new status. Want a drink?"

Elias agreed, and Sully went to fetch a couple of beers from the fridge. Sully needed more information, and this was a perfect time for them to talk about things while Mick and Edward were sleeping. He listened as Elias told him the details about the pact, the faction of demons that wanted in Heaven to destroy it, more about his parents and why the passage must be protected. This passage was to both Heaven and Hell with the means of destroying either kingdom. Sully spoke. "I think I understand now, but for my sake, please tell me how I fit in."

Elias smiled. "A child from both would possess the powers of Hell and Heaven, allowing him entry into either kingdom. This guaranteed the sanctity of protection, but also the child would have the ultimate power to kill both demons and angels. And neither God nor Lucifer would punish the child for such deaths. According to Michael, this would be acceptable for the safety of all. No one knew if the child would be male or female, but the strength of the child would be limitless. I think in time, Sully, you will find your powers growing or may discover more. You have the knowledge of both languages, possess the ability to sense when either fallen angel or demon is near you and will protect both kingdoms. You can't be killed by lower-level demons or angels, which, if I understand correctly about that note and its purpose, will be to your advantage. But a higher demon, like Asteroth or Lucifer, even an archangel can kill you. However, humans cannot kill you. So, you can be killed but just not by your average demon or angel, who might be pissed at you for some reason."

"I can enter Heaven? I already went to Hell. Can I come and go in both kingdoms? Shit, I can die."

Again, Elias smiled. "Yes, you can go freely to both kingdoms. As for dying, I think it will be a long time before a high-level demon or an archangel may kill you. That would break the pact and there will be consequences from both kingdoms. But it is wise to be careful."

Sully took a sip of his beer and noticed that Elias was staring at him. Then Elias pointed at one of the symbols on his arm. "See this one here? This is Lucifer's symbol of life protection for you. None of his servants can harm you. I suppose they can kill you, but you will come back. And this one here? This is the symbol of your father's protection. Then that one here, it's your mother's protection symbol." He noticed Elias kept pointing out all the new tattoos that appeared the minute he accepted his birthright. Sully saw that when Elias pointed to a particular tattoo, he bowed his head for a moment. Then he realized the tattoo was from God.

"This one right here, Sully, is the most sacred of all the heavenly symbols. It means that not only are you protected, but you are blessed."

"Thank you for telling me about my birth. That's the one thing no one has told me. Do you know more?"

Elias smiled and took a sip. "I can do better than that. Let me show you. Just close your eyes. And put down the beer."

Sully did as told and waited. He felt his icy hands on his forehead. Then he saw the images, like a movie. Sully witnessed his mother and father together, holding a baby. His parents went to a village, the same one he grew up in before the monastery. A group of angels and demons were behind his parents but stood in the shadows, not seen. His father gave him to his adopted father while his adopted mother accepted a crucifix from Jophiel. His adopted parents were not afraid of Asmodeus or Jophiel, but both knelt before them. What he saw seemed strange, but it helped explain how he came to be in the village. Sully opened his eyes. This may be one of the few times in which angels and demons were on the same side.

"My parents knew my true nature? They never told me."

"Hunter—Sully, I mean, your parents understood your purpose and the pact. It was explained to them before. They were to keep you safe, send you to the monastery, and wait for you to be ready. Now is the time. You must be ready."

"Don't worry about me. I've been hunting for a very long time. This will be no different. But let's find that map you hid and figure out where we need to go. Mick will be better after some rest. You gained your strength back, too. All you needed was a beer!"

Sully laughed as he said that, slapping his new friend on the back. Elias looked for the book while Sully studied some of the ancient book his father had given him. He wanted to be prepared the best he could. And somehow, deep down, he wanted to make both his parents proud and to show that he was committed to his destiny. There was a page that showed itself to him when he turned to it. It talked about the passage. Could it be the same passage he needed to protect? He read it.

If the passage to Hell is opened, it's not what could gain entry, but what is unleashed. Hellhounds would roam free, finding servants for demons. The hounds would not return to Hell until the last innocent soul was offered to Lucifer. The only one the hounds fear the most is the Hunter. Armed with the Book of Demons, the hellhounds can be mastered by the Hunter alone. The passage can only be closed by the Hunter once it has been opened. It will require the blood of the Hunter to seal the passage. The key to open, the blood to close.

Sully was the hunter that the book referenced. He put

the book aside and grabbed another. This time, it referenced Heaven. Similar text to what he'd read was now visible to him, but it described the passage to Heaven. Sully realized his responsibility to ensure he maintained the balance. He couldn't keep from laughing anymore. It was so loud that it must've caught Elias's attention.

"What's so funny, hunter?"

"I just realized that I am the guardian of angels and the angel of death, so to speak, all rolled in one. That's a lot of shit."

Sully realized Elias got his sense of humor when the man started laughing so loud that he woke up Edward and Mick. The others joined Sully at the table and began examining the parchments, notes, books, everything that was available to them. Elias opened one book and asked for a knife. Once he had the knife, Sully watched him cut into the cover and pull out another parchment.

Not wanting to appear anxious, Sully asked, "Is that the map?"

"Yes, hunter. It is the map of the first garden. This is an ancient parchment. Be gentle with it, but it is not mine. I was only to ensure that it was given to you when the time was right. In addition, you, Mick, are the hunter and the beacon for the key and the passage. I am to ensure that you follow the path on the map to reach the garden. The rest will be for you to discover."

Mick broke the silence. "I'm still trying to piece things together and I'm discovering that I'm... the daughter of Michael, like the archangel Michael. Did you know this, any of you?"

Edward looked in Sully's direction and said, "Brother. We aren't alone."

Sully always could tell when demons were near. His senses have never failed him and though, before he never understood why or how he could sense them, it all made sense now. Through his mother and father. The demon and the archangel.

"I feel their presence. Take Elias and Mick to my room. Watch them and use the vials I have in the nightstand drawer. This is going to get messy."

Sully made them take all the books and parchments with them as they hid. While they did that, he prepared for a bloody fight. He felt the soul eater inside, and together his power amplified. He was ready. Armed with his sword, Sully also reached for the blade he kept in his pocket and looked at his tattoos. He said a prayer, which was becoming a habit before having to fight demons. The soul eater spoke to him.

"Demon assassins. But not from Lucifer. They serve Balam. Breathe. We got this."

He ran his fingers through his blue hair and took a deep breath. He knew that this alliance with the soul eater would benefit not just him but would keep Mick safe somehow. His life had been turned upside down, but it didn't keep him from wondering about the role that Margaret and the organization still played in this. One problem at a time.

The door exploded and was hanging on its hinges. Pieces of wood flew into his apartment. Standing straight in front of him were eight large demons, each armed with their weapon of choice. Sully gripped his sword, using both hands, and shifted his stance between his feet. He was agile and ready for anything.

The demon leader spoke. "Balam wants the prophet. Give him to us and you can live, hunter. In exchange for the prophet, you can have one of us at your side."

Sully laughed. "Which one of you wants to stand by me?"

The leader pushed the female demon Katarina forward. "I believe you two have already met in Hell." He laughed.

Sully took a long look at Katarina and recognized her. Asmodeus had commanded her to keep him in Hell. Or at least try to, but she failed. She was so beautiful. His mind was beginning to get fuzzy the more he looked at her. His head kept slipping as if he was falling asleep. The soul eater sensed Katarina's hold. He forced his way to control Sully, which wasn't hard to do. Sully's eyes flashed open and shot the demons a sharp look of death.

"Know who I am? I inhabit the body of this hunter."

Since Sully had merged with the soul eater, he could feel the changes that took place in his body. He knew that the soul eater was feeding on him, though he tried not to think about it. That was the agreement they'd made. Sully wouldn't be able to explain how, but he could see out of just one eye and the soul eater out of the other. He was becoming accustomed to this new arrangement, although he still could have conversations with the soul eater. That was the one thing that was still a little strange to take in. But the power, the control, the balance—Sully loved every minute. He accepted his destiny and enjoyed the fact that he couldn't be killed by either side. The only thing that frustrated him was keeping the balance, and that was difficult since he'd spent his life hunting and killing demons.

"Soul eater."

"And the demon hunter. We are one. Don't we make a formidable team, Katarina?" Sully couldn't stop laughing at the taunting of her. He saw she had a slight look of fear in her eyes, but she moved towards him, as if to distract him with her body. Sully grabbed her by the waist and kissed her hard before pushing her back towards the demons.

He said, "You can't have the prophet. He's with me, under my protection."

Sully raised his hands, palms toward the demons and was prepared to show them the slightest hint of his newfound power and strength, but it was to no avail. Before he could, the demons had vanished. All save Katarina. He thought perhaps that they were called back to Hell. Lowering his hands, Sully called to the others and suggested that they get moving to go where the map would direct them while he dealt with Katarina.

CHAPTER 22

Katarina strutted towards Sully and while he relished how that felt, he felt a pain as he thought of Mick. He wondered why Katarina hadn't disappeared with the others, so Sully asked her about her intentions. There was no way this demon could be alone with Mick and Elias. Edward could handle himself. Mick and Elias were ill prepared to fight demons. She ran her fingers from Sully's waist up his torso and stopped right under his chin.

"Hunter, your hair. Your body. You changed so much in a short time. I likey," she said in a purring voice.

Sully felt himself pulling towards her, as much as

she was in return, based on body language. Damn, he thought. Being the son of the demon of lust is going to take its toll, but he might try to use this to his advantage. Through one eye, he was seeing her through Sully, while the other one was seeing her through the soul eater. A thought entered his mind, coming from the soul eater: *Take her to the bedroom. Lead her into thinking you trust her. Then, I will take over. Trust me, hunter.*

Reaching for her hand, Sully eased her towards him. He kissed her once more and before anything else could happen, he picked her up and straddled his waist. Still kissing her, he walked over to his bedroom and threw her down on the bed. Sully learned fast about women thanks to embracing his destiny. He was no longer the monk.

Sully closed his eyes and allowed the soul eater to see out of both, meaning he was in control. "Listen up, demon bitch." He saw her eyes look confused and then narrow as if she were angry. "That's right. It's me. Balam wants something from the hunter. That's why you were left behind. What was it? Or I will unleash the full power of the hunter on you and dearie, we are still figuring out his full potential. We don't know what he is capable of, but we can find out while we play with you. You can be my new toy."

Katarina struggled to sit up at first, but then she started talking, more like rambling. As the soul eater listened, he understood Balam's plan and brought Sully back, so both were now in control. Sully asked, "Why is the prophet needed?"

She shrugged and only said that her part was to gain his trust, entice him even into bedding her in return for the return of her soul. Katarina said that she had hoped the hunter would plant his seed in her to control Asmodeus, because Balam knew Asmodeus honored the pact. Balam wanted the pact ended. This made him think of what he still didn't know about the situation. He only had one option: to buy time. And she would become powerful and revered if she carried the hunter's seed.

Katarina spoke more. "They knew that no man or demon could resist me, so Balam wanted to gain control. He had to prove to the other demons that he was the strongest to lead them against Asmodeus and to destroy the pact. All I wanted was to bed the hunter. You don't realize how enticing you are to us, do you?"

He agreed to bedding her, but at the time of his choosing in exchange for everything she knew about Balam and his need to destroy the pact. Though the thought pleased him and yet disgusted him at the same time, he told her she had to tell him everything first and be obedient for how long he saw her use. Sully made sure that she understood he would bed her once, but not father her child. That would be out of the question. Katarina agreed to his terms, and that made him smile. Until he thought of Mick. *Shit, two women. What am I doing?*

Sully told her to join the others, and he planned for the visit to the first garden if they could find it. When Katarina and Sully joined the others, he saw the look of fear in their eyes and reassured them he had a plan and that she was needed. Once he took the time to explain about Balam's plan and how he wanted to use Katarina to control Asmodeus, they seemed to relax a little, but Edward had taken him aside to speak his mind.

"Brother, I don't like this. We don't even know if she can be trusted. Do you trust her? And Balam wants to control father. Why? We should warn him, we should."

Sully cut him off mid-sentence. "Edward, brother, do not fear. You can tell father if you want to. The soul eater has a plan, and I agree with it. We can combine both our plans into one and do what is expected of me. No harm will come to you, brother. I guess I don't acknowledge our relationship as much as I should. Edward, I am sorry. I have accepted my destiny. Forgive me, brother?"

Edward hugged him tight and whispered, "Always."

Sully told Katarina to tell them everything she knew as they sat around the table. Mick fumbled in the kitchen to whip up drinks and snacks for the new team. Elias listened, asking Katarina lots of questions, and before long, Sully realized he would not be alone. He was strong and ready to face what would come. Hours passed and he approached Mick. He needed to talk to her.

"Mick, we need to talk. I am not experienced as you learned, but there's something about you I feel connected to. I was wondering…"

Sully couldn't finish his sentence because Mick pulled him close to her and kissed him hard. His body awakened at her touch and before he could return the kiss, she stopped and screamed. Then his body burned. Both received tattoos. Mick showed him her wrist. Sully looked at his wrist and at hers. They each had the same tattoo. It was a pitchfork and angel wings merged. Sully called for

Elias.

Before Sully could say anything, the entire group was standing in front of both Mick and Sully. Elias smiled when Sully showed him their wrists.

"God and Lucifer have agreed. You two are now bound to each other as hunter and beacon, friends, lovers, as man and wife, in a way. It was written this way when the pact was made at Michael's suggestion, because it would be the only safe way for the key to show itself. It would remain hidden until you both have found each other. Heaven and Hell have spoken. We are nothing more than their servants. It is time. Let's study the map."

Sully shrugged and looked at Katarina. He noticed she appeared to be disappointed, considering what he'd just promised her. Then he stole a quick glance at Mick.

***

Mick was not shocked at the news about Katarina, but she felt a twinge of jealousy. She always sensed that Sully was attractive to all the females, but Katarina was beautiful, seductive and she could relate with his demon side better than she could. Mick really liked Sully and wanted to see things progress, but she wasn't sure about the two of them sleeping together when they weren't even dating. She wanted to and hoped that Sully felt the same. She turned around and headed away from the group, with a tear in her eye.

Sully must've sensed something was wrong because she didn't get far before his hands wrapped around her waist. "I can feel your sadness. Is it because of Katarina?"

Placing her hands around his, she said in a low voice, "I like you. I know you like me. I just want to see where things go when we're ready."

"I choose you, Mick. Not Katarina. That's an agreement to get us what we need. There is nothing between Katarina and me. I promise."

***

He spoke aloud. "Katarina, I gave you my agreement and I will not break my word. But you and I owe it to tell Mick the agreement for your helping us. Mick, in order for things to be learned, I promised to bed Katarina. It would be the only way to get the information on Balam, save my father, and return her soul to her. This was before, well, before this tattoo. I'm sorry."

Sully stared at Mick, longing to be alone with her once more. To finish what they started. His mind and heart were racing at the thought of touching her again, kissing her lips, breathing in her scent. Then he saw Mick's face. It seemed that she was a little upset at something.

Mick said, "This is new to me. You promised to bed her once. Once, demon bitch, is all you will get. Nothing more, nothing less. But your information on Balam better be accurate, or I will call this agreement off. The archangel Michael is my father, and I am my father's daughter. Hear me?"

As she said that in a commanding voice, Sully noticed

that there was an aura all around her. It was strong, and the color was gold. Sully then saw an aura around the others, different colors, different strengths. He realized that the growth of his powers was just starting. The room filled with a powerful light. As the group adjusted their eyes, Sully realized that archangel Michael stood before them. His world was suddenly more entangled with the highest archangel in his apartment and demons surrounding him. Sully just rolled his eyes and fumbled at the words coming out of his mouth.

Michael put his hand up, motioning for silence. He said one word. "Daughter." Sully thought his voice seemed musical for a minute, but then he heard someone else say a similar thing. He looked towards Mick and saw that she was moving closer to Michael.

"Father. I suppose."

Michael smiled and looked at Sully. "When you were born, it was because of a decree. Your place on earth is to protect both kingdoms, angels, demons, and humans. Hunter, I give you this sword. The angel blade and the demon blade, given to you by your father. Do you still have both?"

Sully replied, "Yes. Just call me Sully. Too many are calling me hunter, and I don't know if I like it anymore."

"Good. But you are still the hunter, Sully. Merge them with this sword. It is to replace all other swords you may have. It is meant for you. This sword is from both Heaven and Hell, and you will need it as we learned that the demon factions and now, angel factions, are in league together to find the passage. Take it. You will know when to merge the sword. Prophet. Good to see you, friend. It is by heavenly decree, prophet, that you stay with them. I see you have friends from the other side, too, hunter. Demons, in fact. You need that. Jophiel sends her blessings to you. You must prepare to leave now. First, we need to have an exchange, daughter. Come."

Mick walked towards him, and Sully saw Michael put his hand on her shoulder.

***

Mick knew the others were watching them but she had so many questions for him. Daughter? She felt comfortable with him and safe, but the questions she had just poured out of her mouth. She wasn't afraid of hearing the truth.

"I'm like Sully? How come you waited so long to appear to me and why didn't you save me from my childhood? All those homes, all those horrible foster parents. Why? You were supposed to protect me and you didn't."

Michael took the questions and the upset tone from Mick, but she waited for an answer to come and none did. At last, he put his hand on her head, and spoke.

"Daughter, I was always with you, even in those darkest hours. Trust me, you were never alone. You and Sully have a destiny, a birthright, and that is the greatest gift that could be bestowed upon you both. However, I must insist that you come with me now to learn your part and so that we can get to know each other. What do you think?"

Mick felt a sense of peace coming from him, so she agreed.

***

Before he could say anything, both had disappeared. Sully was surprised how well she was taking all this in, but then again, he had too when he'd learned who he was. It must be in their nature. Elias put his hand on Sully's shoulder, and it comforted him.

"Hunter, she will be back. It's her destiny to stand by your side. But you heard Michael. We must leave."

"Show me the map, Elias. Let's see where we go. Then, I have a new sword to build or merge, whatever Michael wanted me to do. And you, Katarina, will stay by my side. Don't mistake my goodwill for the alliance we have made. Everything else will be in my choosing. I will kill you here and now. Understand me?"

At that moment, Sully was angry and afraid. A lifetime of hunting demons morphed into a new life, one he never asked for. The soul eater must've sensed his frustration and sent him a wave of power, like he usually received. Sully felt calmer and more at ease. He studied the map carefully when Elias pointed out where they needed to go to find the first garden. Sully was very gentle with the parchment as he turned it in a different direction to get a closer look. Centuries of wandering the world made him understand map reading when it came to finding demons. It was how he got around.

"Elias, there's no known history of the exact location of the garden in the world. But this parchment shows a location for Eden. I don't believe it. It's right here. I see it, but I think I'm so surprised that there's a map that I'm nervous to say where we are going."

Elias started laughing. Sully was warned not to tell where they were going because he was unsure about Katarina's new purpose. Sully had to consider that carefully because she was with the demons who served Balam. He was losing confidence with so many demon factions now and the sides they were taking. All Sully wanted was to learn his destiny and fulfill it to protect Heaven and Hell. The demons would align themselves with him as much as the angels would. He pulled Katarina aside but made sure that Edward and Elias could hear her words.

"Katarina, I warned you once before. Now, I am going to tell you I will trust you as long as you remain true to your word. Remember, I will feel nothing if I have to kill you and send you back to Hell, soulless and beaten by the hunter."

Katarina nodded and extended her hand for him the shake. Sully thought to himself, *Great, another unholy alliance.*

CHAPTER 23

It took a few weeks to make the travel plans for the group, but eventually Sully and his new team found their way with the guidance of the old parchment. Sully had spent centuries wandering the world since leaving the monastery, but he never knew about this secret location of the garden. He'd practically visited every country, but somehow, coming to 'old Mesopotamia' was not something he did. Today, however, the land was known as Iraq, and this made things slightly challenging. The one thing about demons was that most could blend in but it would be very hard to explain his weaponry.

The group made their way across the dry land, survived the heat and eventually, Elias led them. For the last several days, Sully took the time to get to know Katarina. She was beautiful, but he missed Mick greatly. He noticed Edward tried his best to cheer him up, but his mind was still on Mick. Sully asked the others to set up a camp for the night but to prepare it for anything. He had an unexplainable feeling that things were not going to be easy in the desert. Sully left for a bit to pray. He prayed to Michael and to God for her safe return to him, as well as the safety of the group. Never wanting to be selfish, Sully apologized for praying for himself, but he felt lost and needed guidance.

As one, Sully knew that the soul eater sensed his fear and hopelessness, but he was so tired that he drifted off to sleep. Then he dreamt. He saw Mick and Michael. She looked so happy, but Michael was persuading her to return to Sully. Her path, her destiny, was already chosen years ago. He felt like he was eavesdropping on the conversation, but it was just his dream. Sully realized that Mick and he were together. Michael then appeared to him. He placed his hand on Sully's shoulder and whispered in his ear. That's when Sully fully woke.

It took a few moments for his senses to return but once they did, he assessed the area and his friends. Thanks to Michael's warning, Sully was able to prepare for Balam. Balam was coming. Sully shouted for Edward to get ready. He questioned if Katarina had betrayed them, but when he looked for her, she was sound asleep by Elias though it was early night. Elias took no chances to leave her alone if Sully was not attached to her somehow.

Sully silently whispered to the soul eater. Lately, he didn't feel the soul eater feeding on his soul, but this time, he did. Maybe he was just too tired with everything going on. And there had been no sign of Margaret either. Reaching for his sword, he clasped it tightly in two hands. Raising it first to the sky in reverence to Heaven, he then pointed the tip towards to ground, also in reverence for Hell. That's when he knelt on one knee, grabbed hold of his crucifix, and cried. He ran his fingers over all his tattoos and yelled once, "Give me the strength of both Heaven and Hell to do my eternal duty!" Using the blades, he merged his sword. The weapon of his birthright. His destiny. Light erupted from the sword while flames surrounded Sully. From the sky, a loud thunder shook the sky as if it answered Sully's plea. Then all was dark again.

Before he could rise, Balam stood near their camp.. The others were struggling to rise as a horde of demons surrounded them. The demon king approached Sully. Sully found the strength on his own to rise to his feet. He sheathed his sword and vowed vengeance on the demon.

Balam laughed and raised his finger towards Sully's chin. He floated in the air and landed hard on the earth when Balam lowered his finger. The demons that surrounded the group kept them occupied while Sully was under attack. That's when he heard Edward scream for Lucifer, not Asmodeus. His body heated, his heart beating faster, and he felt something like a power surge flow through him. The moon was out, and Sully could see two mountains in the distance. As Balam kept attacking him, his one eye focused on the mountains and he wondered if that was what Mick was saying when she was mumbling. Before he could figure that out, Balam pulled him towards him with a powerful force that there was nothing Sully could do to free himself.

Then, by some miracle, daylight was breaking—except that it wasn't time for the sun to rise. The sun eventually reached the moon, and it was beautiful. The moon and the sun touched in the sky. As they did so, a heavenly light came down while, at the same time, a red light rose from under the earth and covered Sully. Sully was covered in light by both Heaven and Hell while the ground shook. Sully, aided with the power of the soul eater, gripped his sword once more and raised it, yelling, "I AM THE PROTECTOR OF HEAVEN AND HELL" in the loudest voice he could muster.

The two lights continued to surround him, but the pull from Balam was broken. Pointing his sword at the horde of demons, Sully sent them back to Hell in mere seconds. Then he faced Balam.

"Demon King, Balam, or whatever the fuck you are, I have accepted my duty to the agreement between Heaven and Hell. You will not take the key today. I banish you back to Hell. Come, fight me another day, demon. I am not just the hunter anymore. Call me the protector. I am the chosen one by both God and Lucifer. Fear me, demon." And when he pointed the sword towards Balam, it was too late. Balam had disappeared on his own.

The light that covered Sully had now disappeared, and

the others stood up and hugged each other. Sully smiled. They were alive for now, but he knew their journey was far from over. Looking for Katarina, he saw her looking disheveled and confused. He gave her a smile and nodded in her direction. She must've noticed because she returned the smile. He hugged Edward and slapped Elias on the back. That's when he pointed towards the two mountains and said, "That's where we will find the garden and hopefully the key."

As they walked toward the mountains, a familiar figure came toward them. It was Mick. Sully ran to her and, as he lifted her in the air, he gave her a kiss. A hard kiss. Sully forgot they were not alone as he caressed her body. That's when he noticed the others walked ahead, leaving the two alone.

Sully could not express how much he missed her in words, so he let his hands do the talking. He rubbed his them up and down her body, feeling every inch and curve. One hand lifted her shirt, reaching under to caress her breasts. Mick did not stop him. He had no experience, but he let lust rule his body. He was the son of Asmodeus. The demon of lust. Kissing her cheeks, his mouth moved farther down her neck, in between her breasts and down her stomach. Sully didn't care that they were outside in the dirt. He gently removed her clothes and opened her legs to let him in. Using a gentle rhythm, he took her, made her moan until they both exploded with intensity and ecstasy. After a while, they got dressed and started walking.

Mick reached for Sully's hand as they caught up to the others. Upon reaching them, Sully noticed that both Edward and Elias were smiling. Katarina was quiet until she noticed a car heading towards them at a fast rate. It was just a matter of seconds before Sully recognized the car, not to mention the feeling he had. Margaret. His day was not getting better. And then he remembered being told that angels and demons were going to come after them once they headed for the garden.

Damn. Here we go again, he thought. After the fight with Balam, Sully hadn't fully recovered his power, but he sucked it up and prepared his mind. His muscles were aching, but he shook that feeling off. He saw Margaret come out of the car with her minions.

"Sully. I see you are on your way to the key. My offer stands for you to join us, or I will be forced to shoot."

Sully told the group to find cover and not move. He told Mick that he must stop this. They had a duty. The others tried to find cover, but Sully stood in place. Then he inched forward, towards Margaret. Slowly, he made his way. Step by step.

"I will not join you. I know who I am. And I know what you really want. You will never get it."

He saw Margaret motion for one of her minions to shoot at them. And they did. The bullet found its way into Elias. Sully watched as his friend collapsed on the ground. Rage built inside him. He unleashed that anger, through his hands, towards Margaret's minions. One by one, they were set aflame. Then he whispered, "Forgive me for what I am about to do."

Sully closed his eyes, took the deepest of breaths and yelled to her in Gaelic. Once he finished his curse, Margaret fell to the ground and screamed. He didn't kill her, just paralyzed her permanently. The only way she would get around now is with a wheelchair, unless she had a way to improve her condition, which he doubted. He felt such anger and betrayal toward her that he wanted to make sure she could never easily follow him again. He laughed and yelled at her once more. "Catch us if you can, bitch."

Knowing that Elias was wounded, he ran to his friend. Elias was still alive, but he had to stop the bleeding. That's when Mick spoke to him. "Take him to the garden. Can you carry him?"

Sully threw him over his shoulder and carried him towards the mountains. They walked for a few hours until they reached the base. Sully noticed the markings near one entrance. It was marked with a heavenly symbol. He could feel it in his bones. The group had reached the gardens. Elias' breathing was getting fainter and fainter. Sully knew there was not much time left. He pushed on into the mountain. The walls were covered with symbols that glowed. He felt the holiness of this place. Finally, they reached the other end of the mountain.

Sully told the others to stay put. He wanted to go in first to save Elias.

"Brother, I will be ok. Stay here and guard the women. I will be back once I save Elias."

Sully walked into the garden. It was just as beautiful as described in the Bible. The birds were in the trees; the animals were roaming the green earth and a sense of peace filled the air. Sully was in a trance, but then realized Elias had little time left. He continued to walk into the center of the garden and laid Elias down on the soft, green grass. Sully got down once more on his knee and prayed for his friend.

"Lord, hear my prayer. I am and always will be your faithful servant. I bring you one of your children, Elias. My friend, the bartender, your prophet. I will surrender to you to save his life. That is all I ask."

Before Sully could get up, Michael and several other archangels, including Jophiel, appeared.

"My son. Rise. Elias will live. But there is a price. Remember what I told you. You cannot serve just one side. You must serve both sides, always. In this garden is the key. Mick will guide you to the key. Use the key to keep the passage closed. But that is not your only duty. The factions are coming from both sides. You will be forced to kill both sides to keep the passage closed. War between the factions and the ones you are bound to protect is inevitable."

Sully nodded. "I will serve and protect both sides. Angels and Demons. And Elias?"

An angel approached Elias and healed his mortal wounds. Sully said something but stopped when he heard the others approaching the center. It was Katarina, Mick, and Edward. That's when Michael broke the silence.

"A formidable team on both sides. Just as God and Lucifer agreed to eons ago. Your journey has just begun. The garden is yours to use, but once you get what you came for, you will need to leave. The garden will not open again until the factions are stopped. You will heal here, so rest until your strength returns." Michael walked towards the others but stopped and turned to face Sully once more. Smiling, he said, "But do not eat the apple. That has never changed since the beginning of creation."

Sully couldn't help himself but laugh and the others joined in.

CHAPTER 24

Elias was showing signs of improvement and Mick appeared to come to terms with her given destiny. Sully was at peace, or at least as much as he could be considering his plight and what lay ahead of them. More demons. More angels. Factions from both sides. But he knew that the garden would not be available to them much longer. He needed the key. He had to speak to Elias.

"Elias, friend and prophet. We need to find the key. We can't stay in the garden much longer. Are you strong enough?"

Elias looked up at Sully, and as his eyes turned white,

he said, "Find the tree with the forbidden fruit. Do not touch nor eat the fruit. Instead, look at the base of the trunk where you will see the symbol of the Lord. It should match one of your tattoos. Dig there for the key. I had to hide the key once I took it from the demons to protect the gates of Heaven. Bring the key back and we will leave the first garden."

Sully instructed Edward and Katarina to stay with Elias while he and Mick went to look for this particular tree. He knew the story of creation and it was one of his favorite Bible passages, but to actually be in the first garden was a miracle. He knelt down and prayed. It was his duty and obligation to respect the garden.

Mick reached for his hand when he was done.

"What happens after we find the key?"

"I'm not sure. I know we will have to make sure that no demon enters Heaven, at the very least. I have a bone to pick with some though but that will have to wait. I'm not sure where we go from here, but I do know that we must stick together. And I was commanded by Michael to remain at your side."

Mick agreed and started to jog to find the tree. It was the largest tree in the center of the garden. It was magnificent and majestic, so large that Sully had to strain to see how tall it was. Not touching anything on the tree, he found the symbol that Elias described. Kneeling down at the base, he began to dig. He dug until his fingers touched something hard and cold. Scooping it up with his hands, he held it up for Mick to see. It was the key. It was a rusted color, but it was the key.

As he held the key in the light, he noticed the faintest inscription. He couldn't read it all, but he recognized the symbols of being from both the angelic and demonic languages. Remembering that he was told that the key was forged by demons, something was amiss. Either the prophecy was wrong, or his responsibilities were now worse. Sully had the key that would open the passages to both Heaven and Hell. He felt a knot in his stomach, knowing that he and the others would have to leave the safety of the garden to return to the rest of humanity and the unknown, when it came to the factions. He was, after all, the sworn protector of Heaven and Hell now. And factions were coming after the key.

As they made their way back to the others, he couldn't contain his excitement to show the key to them, especially to Elias. Elias smiled as he stood up. He found a large stick to use as a cane and handed it to Elias. Sully, for the first time, understood who he was. The son of Asmodeus and Jophiel. His group of protectors were ready to leave the garden behind to face the factions that were bent on seeing the world destroyed.

As the group headed away from the mountain, Edward ran to Sully's side, tugging at him. Sully whispered, "Keep walking. I sense them too. I smell them. I need you to take Mick and Katarina to safety when they appear. Just don't bring them to Hell. Can you do that for me, brother?"

He noticed that Edward was thoughtful and quiet. He began to wonder if Edward somehow devised a different plan while he and Mick were off getting the key.

"Yes, Sully. We are in this together."

***

Edward had to think for a moment about where he could take them. He only relied on Asmodeus when things got difficult. He was sorry to break his promise to his brother, but he had no other choice. In a soft voice, he called out.

"Father, help me. I promised Sully to save the girls. He needs your help. I need your help in order to help Sully."

Asmodeus answered his cry for help. "Son, bring them to Hell. When it is time, bring them here. I have a plan for you but it means you will be away from Sully for a while. I will explain when you bring them here. I will let his mother know where the girls are and that will be our secret. She and I have never kept secrets from each other and I'm not about to start now."

Edward got ready with a new plan, even if it meant disobeying his brother. But in the end, his job was to keep them safe.

***

Moments later, Sully said in a loud voice, "Edward, *now!* Elias, come with me."

There wasn't much time after he said that before he was fighting again. This time it was another horde of demons led by Asteroth. Sully reached for his sword and prepared for battle. He was aware that Elias was not a fighter, but he was surprised when Elias took up a fighting stance. Sully shrugged it off considering where Elias lived, and he was a bartender. The first three demons were no match for Elias because as he watched, Elias used a powerful spell that knocked them over. He even saw Elias smile at the feat he'd just witnessed.

Face to face with a lower demon, Sully enticed him.

"Want to play, demon?" Sully laughed at his own humor, while the soul eater was just hungry for fighting. He decided to let the soul eater have a little fun. After all, they were in this together and there was no turning back now.

The demon showed no fear. *This is going to be easy,* thought Sully.

"Hunter. I've been waiting for my chance to destroy you."

The next time Sully blinked his eyes, he gave the soul eater full control so that he was looking out both eyes, not just one. The demon's face changed. He must've recognized the soul eater. Sully was amused. The fear in the demon's eyes radiated such pleasure from Sully. He decided to toss his sword hand to hand, creating extra time for the demon to wish he stayed in Hell. At least that's what Sully told himself. Then the soul eater spoke.

"Little demon. Little demon. Come out and play." His voice was tauntingly horrifying. He knew it was his voice, but it came from the soul eater and the sound made Sully cringe. He noticed that the fear in the demon was still there, though he tried not to show it by shifting left and right.

The demon lunged at Sully and missed because he

backed up, teasing the demon more. The snarl from the demon only made him laugh even more. With a flick of his wrist, the sword cut the demon in half and as he held it up, it glistened in the sunlight, blood dripping down the blade.

The soul eater whispered to Sully that he loved this new weapon, forged in the heat of both Heaven and Hell. Sully laughed out loud for a moment, forgetting his current situation. Then he did something that was not in his control—he took his finger and tasted a drop of a blood. The drop on his tongue made him shiver in disgust and he knew this was something the soul eater did. Swallowing hard, he let the soul eater have his tiny moment of satisfaction before saying anything.

"Is that a compliment, soul eater?"

"Yes, hunter. We make a great team."

The soul eater, in full control, annihilated the remaining demon horde by simply sending them back to Hell. It was too easy of a battle. Or was it a distraction? Sully couldn't tell when he gained control of his body through another blink of an eye. Sully made his way to Asteroth. He showed the weapon of choice to Asteroth, who in turn smiled.

Sully and Asteroth entangled in a heated moment. Asteroth punched Sully, sending him backwards several feet, landing hard on the ground. Sully gripped his sword tighter and returned to face Asteroth. Asteroth raised his palm and sent a fireball that he barely dodged. He was beginning to think that he was no match for the demon. Two more fireballs came toward him, the last one hitting him square in the chest, knocking the sword out of his hand and him flat on his back once more.

"Let me have control, hunter. Once more."

"No, I need to see what I am capable of. Asteroth is a strong demon. But I…we are stronger. Remember, the unholy alliance. Demon hunter and soul eater. Join me, but I am in control. And no more tasting blood!"

The soul eater and Sully found a way to combine their strength once more, but this time, with Sully in control. Sully found the strength to stand up and extended his hand, calling for the sword. The sword, now glowing in both gold and black, rose upward from the ground and found its way back to his hand. Turning his wrist in a circular motion, Sully motioned the sword in different angles so that Asteroth could see his fine weapon.

"Asteroth, behold the sword from both Heaven and Hell. Taste my power, feel my wrath. Dance with me, demon?"

Asteroth attempted once more to strike at Sully but this time he was prepared. The symbols on his body, representing both the power of Heaven and Hell combined, began all turn to red. Sully could feel the rage, the power of both kingdoms and he raised one hand, palm facing toward the demon. He felt the power of the soul eater through his body. He was ready.

"Impero tibi vi Lucifer et Deus. Revertere ad inferos."

Asteroth remained there for a moment. Just long enough to leave Sully one message.

"I will return, hunter. This isn't my defeat. I got what I came for. Give my regards to your father." Asteroth vanished, leaving Sully and Elias alone.

Sully was confused and tried to sort out what he meant by that, until he realized that Edward lay on the ground. He hadn't made it to safety with Katarina or Mick. But neither woman was nearby either. Running to Edward, he lifted his head and cradled it in his lap. A tear fell from his cheek and landed on Edward. Using his free hand, he closed Edward's eyes and whispered a prayer. He then sensed it, just like he could with other demons for centuries. Edward wasn't dead, not in the mortal sense. The body was just that of a child. No demon. Edward was gone but how? He vowed revenge on Asteroth for doing this, but he felt Elias' hand on his shoulder. He was glad that his brother wasn't *really* dead. *But where'd they go?*

"You can't avenge him, hunter. Remember the balance. You will destroy the world and Heaven and Hell if you lose that. We will grieve for your brother and find a way to honor him with the balance. Pray with me, hunter. For your brother."

Sully prayed as he did so, Asmodeus appeared. As Sully looked up to his father, he apologized. "Father, I failed you again."

"No, son. Edward is safe. He asked for help earlier and sought a distraction. He knew he wasn't strong enough for what you needed. Yes, he's a demon child, but much smarter than you gave him credit for. He knew something would happen and he brought the women to me for safety while we devised a ruse to weed out the factions. I gave my word long ago to protect you and your destiny no matter the cost. I also gave your mother my solemn vow to let no harm come to you, if it is in my power to control. It will cost me an uprising in Hell, but I can deal with that. What it couldn't cost me would be your failure at your destiny and the destruction of the pact.

"Edward will return to your side, but not as a child. He will be able to fight alongside you for what is yet to come. Travel safe until he returns to you. I will send the women back to you. Just remember, you may be your mother's son, but you are also your father's son. My son. And I am the demon prince. I cannot stay, my son. If you and Elias do not hurry, I'm afraid the gates to Heaven will be opened sooner rather than later. Then the gates of Hell would be next. Once both are open, something awful will be unleased. It is time to search the book. It will guide you once more, my son. Give my love to your mother when you see her again."

Sully knelt before his father, showing signs of fealty and promise that he would do everything in his power to prevent the passage to both Heaven and Hell from opening. With that, Asmodeus bowed to his son, and that's when Sully realized that the task ahead was not finished. It was only starting.

ABOUT THE AUTHOR

Barb Jones currently lives in Sarasota County, Florida with her family and several pets. She earned a bachelor's degree in Political Science and English, followed by a master's degree in Information Systems and Accounting and Finance. When she isn't writing, she's usually enjoying the various activities that Florida has to offer. Her love of the paranormal and horror began when she was a child, growing up in Hawaii. She keeps to her roots when writing. Feel free to reach out to Barb anytime – barb@thebloodprophecy.net as she loves to hear from her readers. You can also sign up for her newsletter by visiting www.thebloodprophecy.com

www.ingramcontent.com/pod-product-compliance
Lightning Source LLC
Chambersburg PA
CBHW010727310726
48971CB00009B/2769